WAVES OF MUTILATION

Sarah Jane Huntington

VELOX BOOKS
Published by arrangement with the author.

CONTENTS

INTRODUCTION

I have always adored short stories. I love full-length novels and novellas too, of course, but short tales seem to impact me more.

Sometimes reading and writing them feels like being the character Sam in the old TV show, *Quantum Leap*, the man who could jump into bodies at important moments in others lives and glimpse that particular reality for a time.

Or maybe it's the equivalent of eating little slices of several differently flavored cakes instead of eating a whole cake? Who am I kidding though, I'd eat the lot.

Either way, I love short stories.

Some of these tales are longer than the ones I would usually write, but the words kept on coming and so I didn't stop.

I like to try and write unique stories, subjects, or approaches that haven't been done before. Sometimes this backfires, and sometimes it works. I am never sure.

I appreciate my writing isn't for everyone. I fully understand that, and I for one, am extremely glad we are all so vastly different and have varied tastes.

This is a miscellaneous collection too. Space, crime, folklore, weird horror, ancient things under the earth and above. I have tried to include story notes at the end of some, to attempt to explain what might have inspired me, but sometimes, I have no idea what sparks a concept.

Please do be aware that suicide is mentioned in this book. Not described, only mentioned, and there are swear words, a small amount of gore, and a damaging mother/ daughter relationship.

It is not and never will be my intention to cause a person upset in any way. Although I write about the dark sides of humanity, I fully understand there is also plenty of light. I expect it might be currently stuck down the back of the sofa is all ;)

Once again, thank you to the wonderful people who are now firm friends in the writing community who have helped me greatly.

As always, I hope you enjoy this book or at least one story and if you are reading this now; I appreciate it more than you can ever imagine.

Much love,
Sarah Jane
Twitter: @SarahJaneHunti1

NO STARS INSIDE DARK HEARTS

Location- Nearing Neptune.
Date- 2034
Ship- Class Cx vessel, The Asimov
Purpose- Planetary scout.

At first, Commander Alice Ramirez feels as if she is falling.

Down and down her stomach and mind plummets, while she herself remains frozen where she stands. She wonders if all those named Alice are prone to falling down mysterious dark holes. Except there are no smartly dressed white rabbits running late for her to chase.

The scanners of her ship are lying.

What she is bearing witness to is nothing but an illusion. An impossibility, or at the very least, a wild malfunction. Again. Such a dangerous glitch might mean the end of the mission.

"This has to be false readings," she finds herself saying. "Or... data corruption."

She believes her own words simply because she does not believe in impossible things. She is a woman of science, proof, and facts. She likes control and smooth, drama-free space travel. Easy routes and mapped out zones.

"Commander, MIND can't be wrong this time," the ship's pilot, Andrew, answers. He is a tall and baby-faced man with exceptional flying skills. He once navigated a small space shuttle through a tiny yet dangerous asteroid field. Not a day goes by when he doesn't mention his amazing feat and enviable skills.

Alice often wonders why he didn't just fly around the hazard.

And of course, the computer system *can* be wrong, can't it?

"An unknown energy shut down our Ion drives. It's all offline," Andrew says. "MIND won't reboot. A force hit like an EMP. The system registered something but... I can't tell what exactly."

"Is that what it was?" She asks. "An electromagnetic pulse?"

"No."

"But MIND is still down?"

"Yes, or at least, partially."

"Will we lose gravity?" She asks.

She hates the feeling of floating around like an untethered, helium-filled balloon. For her, zero gravity was always the very worst part of astronaut training.

"I don't think so; life support is running, according to the system."

The system, the integrated machine.

MIND.

It is the onboard hive-minded computer system responsible for life on board the scout ship, The Asimov, and each piece of essential equipment. Sometimes it behaves as if it has a real, human brain of its own. The system is the first of its kind, the highest branch of artificial technology.

Ion drives are the very best of terrestrial technology too.

They would not be in space at all if it wasn't for computers. Every astronaut is a slave to the wired minds of machines.

"Run diagnostics again, there must be a serious system fault. No, better yet, get me a visual," Alice demands. "Let's see for ourselves that nothing is out there. No black hole, no anything."

Multiple sensors and outside cameras can never, in her opinion, function better than human eyes.

Besides, humanity has been traveling the solar system for a decade, much slower than those in charge would like, yes, but making good progress all the same.

Unknown energy has never once been detected and the great minds of the space program claim they know all there is to know. Even the mysteries of dark matter have been partially unraveled, or so they claim.

And she does not, for a moment, doubt the Ion drives capability to be brought back online.

But, if MIND is failing, it means we'll have to return home, Alice thinks. *Which means less pay.*

She must do her best to avoid such a return trip.

Conditions on Earth are hostile at best. The only decent life a person can possess is inside the glass city domes. Giant snow globes filled with humanity cover the remains of the old and ruined cities. Very likely built upon the bones of thousands of dead. Dome life is bitterly expensive, but to live any other way only invites a slow and brutal end.

The future everyone once dreamed of, of flying cars, world peace, no corruption, and equality for all, failed miserably.

Alice is currently standing on the flight deck, pacing, still half asleep, with one foot in each world, toppling between reality and dreams. She pinches herself to make sure she is awake.

She'd been dreaming of home again, all that fake, yet convincing green grass, recycled air, shiny tall buildings, and her life inside one of the main city domes. Inside her small apartment, she has a single fish in a tank. The fish is mechanical, a fraud, a liar fish. Yet in her sleep, she worried that it wouldn't be fed, as if it ever needed such a thing as food.

Andrew woke her with an engine issue and set her heart cascading.

"MIND detected unknown energy and we're floating towards it. Our power has failed. I think it's possible a black hole is very near."

A sentence no commander ever wanted to hear.

At first, she'd believed her strange dreams might have switched to a nightmare. But no, here she stands. At a loss.

They cannot be powerless in the vastness of space. They have a clear and direct route and not once have they deviated.

It's not as if space is signposted. Constellations, moons, and planets are used as maps and guides.

They are the equivalent of ancient mariners, sailors braving the treacherous oceans countless years before them in the name of discovery and new worlds to conquer.

Currently, they should be nearing the edge of their own solar system, close to Neptune, and en route to a promising Earth-like planet beyond.

Finding a viable new home is of the greatest importance.

Except, there seems to be a problem of some magnitude.

"Why can't MIND compute what's out there?"

"I don't know," Andrew replies. "Hence the unknown aspect, obviously."

Alice ignores his dry attempt at sarcasm.

"You make no sense," she snaps. "None at all."

She feels her stomach clench tightly. She can tell a tension headache is coming on, no doubt brought on by frustration and worry.

"Hold on," he announces. "Visual in five. I think this is what MIND tried to warn us of, before I mean."

Yes, and what did Alice do? She ignored such a warning.

She counts down the valuable seconds; it gives her brain a respite, something to focus on besides the problem she faces.

We'll see familiar constellations and no black holes. Everything is fine. It's a glitch. There's nothing out there but space.

Five, four, three, two...

"On screen, Commander."

There. The vision streaming in from outside fills her eyes.

What the...

Alice falls further down the metaphorical hole.

The sight is utterly incomprehensible. A vast wall of color stands almost directly in front of their ship. Vivid lilacs and subtle shades of blue shine with fierce power. It seems to stretch for eternity, and perhaps it does. Above, below, left, and right. An energy field of the likes no one ever imagined. It flickers like pretty northern lights or campfire flames. Dancing in a design of its own curious making.

The ship is insignificant against it. The equivalent of a tiny drop of saltwater in the largest of oceans.

Where the hell did that come from?

Tendrils of color, like the limbs of an octopus, move and caress the ship gently, as if exploring or tasting.

"What is this?" Alice asks.

"I don't know."

Outside sensors lock onto an object and focus with the sharp clarity of an expert sniper.

Caught in the vast energy cloud is another vessel; it looks so tiny that it could be a child's abandoned toy. Andrew spots it too, he frowns and zooms the camera closer.

Alice feels a shockwave of horror; the sensation spreads until she feels her mind fizz.

The vessel is the lost exploration ship, The Sagan, named after the great astronomer. Beside it is another scout ship just like theirs, The Clarke, named after the author and futurist.

"What!" Alice cries. "It can't be."

But yet, it is.

Both ships out there floating abandoned like ancient silent derelicts. A graveyard of failed exploration. Their shiny surfaces and outer shells are pitted and corroded. As if they have been floating dormant for centuries or millennia.

In reality, contact was lost with The Sagan two years ago. Alice had been present at the launch. She'd watched with great envy; they were the first. They would be the ones who would be remembered. Who recalled the names of those that followed in second or third place? No one, that's who.

And The Clarke, the ship should still be busy scouting for habitable planets.

She is not asleep and not dreaming. Her situation is not a nightmare of epic proportions; it is her cold and brutal reality and she is immediately afraid.

How quickly existence can change in an instant.

"When was The Sagan lost?" Andrew asks.

"A couple of years ago," she says. "MIND, please. What is this energy?"

MIND cannot compute. Will not.

"Get us away," she orders. "Now."

"I can't!"

Alice slaps her palm down onto a single red button. Emergency alert. A fast and loud alarm begins to sound that will wake the remaining crew. A terrible sound to wake up to. The speed of the noise matches her racing heartbeat.

The Asimov is a scout vessel. They have one mission, one journey to their set destination point, and one voyage back. Easy, simple.

It is why she was given command. Scouting for planets is considered uncomplicated. Essential yes, but still, easier than freight or salvage vessels and far easier than scientific research trips.

Alice sits at the head of the table in the rec room, the one they use for leisure or chess, and gazes at the shocked faces staring back at her. They each look to her to know what to do. She has no answers, only sharp fear, deep ripples of unease. Her skin prickles violently and why is it so warm and stuffy?

She longs for someone to step up and tell her what to do.

I'm in charge. Me. Be responsible.

"We appear to be in unknown territory," she says. "Somehow, we've run into a serious issue. The Ion drives are down. We're caught in some kind of energy. The ship is drifting towards a…"

She does not know how to finish her sentence.

"Can this be a navigational error?" Mack asks. "Are we sure we are where we should be?"

Mack is the oldest member of the crew. He has years of experience under his belt. His mind is quick, calm, and clever, and yet he clearly isn't listening.

He has a long beard peppered with bright white streaks. Alice sees that he has a small chunk of food trapped among the gray. The sight makes her mind feel itchy.

Should she say something? Is it really the right time? Her thoughts scramble and she almost laughs.

"No navigation error," Andrew says and snaps her back to reality.

"Our route appeared to be clear. MIND detected unknown energy and something out there shut down our full power. Life support is running; inside comms are active. The cameras too. That field of color just appeared."

"How can you tell MIND isn't malfunctioning again?"

"I can tell and it looks like MIND didn't malfunction near Uranus after all. Besides, look out of the window."

No one speaks. Alice feels her cheeks flame with fresh heat.

The heavy judgment and silence becomes so loud that she coughs, just for something to hear. She has peered out of the window countless times already, at every angle possible. The vision outside is unknown and terrifying. She can sense its menace, or imagines she can.

It has bad intentions.

"Whatever it is has caught us and the other ships up like a spider's web."

This time, it is Sophie who speaks.

Brave and sweet Sophie, the best engineer in the space program. People always said that there was nothing she couldn't fix if she had the right tools. Alice feels lucky to have her.

She feels as if her skin is growing hotter. Something is happening that she can't explain. There is danger; she can sense it on a primal level. Her hands become sweaty and itchy.

The chunk of food in Mack's beard becomes all she can think about. She wants to scream.

She wonders if she is the equivalent of a fork in a room of human spoons. She did always feel that way, the odd one out, different in shape and in function.

Mohammed leans back in his chair and taps his pen. She feels a brief spark of hope. He is smart, a genius really. He has a rational way of thinking she admires. If anyone can determine what might have occurred, it will be him.

"Space," he begins, "Is still very uncharted."

"We've been traveling our solar system for years! Nothing like this has ever happened," Mack interrupts.

Mohammed holds up a single hand. He has enough respect and authority to bring quick silence to the room.

"An entire ocean cannot be judged by a handful of sea crossings. Besides, we're on the edge of our solar system. Clearly, we've run into some kind of discrepancy. Perhaps it's an energy wave or something new. Anti-matter? We've never traveled this far. The ships before us have yes, but I think we know what became of them now. Perhaps time is a factor too."

Alice glances at her watch. She can't think what he means. She is finding his words hard to follow and harder to focus on.

"But probes," Sophie says. "Since Voyager, hundreds of probes have passed beyond Neptune."

She raises a good point, one Alice herself hadn't considered. Yet, what does it mean?

"Why doesn't MIND know what it is?" Andrew says. "Why didn't The Clarke warn us? There have been no distress signals at all."

All eyes look to Mohammed for the answer.

"Maybe they had no transmitting power. MIND has no concept or awareness of what it *is* out there. The system is only programmed and given the knowledge *we* have. That energy is entirely unknown. Beyond our comprehension too, no doubt. And perhaps, although only perhaps, time might run faster the closer we get. I believe MIND may have picked it up, near Uranus and warned us in the only way it knew how. We did not react in time or…"

This time, Alice looks harder at her watch. She understands Mohammed's words on one level, but she can't think what the connections might mean. She feels sure she used to know.

The room remains silent. She imagines she can hear the ticking of brains trying to work out the science or the math, the implications of such new and dangerous space hazards.

"What about the crew on other ships?" Sophie asks.

"They're likely dead," Mohammed answers. "We should log this, contact mission control, and ask for further instructions."

"We're out of range," Andrew reminds everyone. "We could message the ships behind us if I can get outside comms online. If I can't, they'll have no idea."

If that's happened to us, it must have happened to the other ships.

It's so obvious; she curses herself for not thinking of such a thing before.

Why can't I think straight?

She blinks rapidly. She feels terrified. She should feel interested, even excited. There could be answers inside the energy field that have eluded the greatest physicists on Earth for centuries and yet she doesn't want to go near the ships that are tangled up inside. They are a scout vessel, the lowest of the low in the world of space travel. Low and expendable.

"Suggestions?" She asks. She has none of her own.

"I could try to bypass MIND and get the Ion drives working. Or at least one."

"Do it, Sophie."

Alice stands and walks a few steps until she faces the only window in the room. It is a thick and tiny porthole view and enough for her to see out into the great void.

It is impossible to believe that only one wall stands between her and frozen death.

Space. It really is unimaginably endless. Stars she never gets to see from Earth shine like pretty glitter caught in the sun.

The field of color takes up the majority of her view. The swirls of lilacs are moving, rippling. As if the energy is constantly changing or alive somehow. She squints and sees a grid shine briefly. For a moment, it looks like lines intersect in a complex pattern.

Is this a natural construct or not?

After years of humanity venturing out into the solar system, no civilization or traces of an alien race have ever been found. There have been rumors, as there always have been. Still, world governments have remained tight-lipped on the subject or issued statements of full denial.

It has to be some form of natural energy, and what happened to the people on those ships?

"Commander," Andrew says. "What shall we do?"

"What? Oh."

It is her responsibility to issue orders. The ship is under her command, she almost forgot. Yes, they do travel for set purposes but also for exploration reasons if the need arises.

"Concentrate on fixing the Ion drives first. Let me think."

Except Alice does not want to think. She wants to lie in her narrow bed and cease to exist.

The control she cherishes has fallen from her grip. She is a boat without an anchor. The pounding inside her head steadily increases.

She knew the journey must be cursed. They all did. Close to Uranus, near the cold moon Umbriel, the whole crew felt damned and agitated. Of course, MIND's sudden warning was what started the whole episode.

***

She was sleeping when the system began to play a cacophony of wild alarms. The most dreadful sound to wake up to. She went sprinting to the flight deck, crashing into a panicking Mack as she fled.

"Micro Asteroids?" He yelled. "Is that what this is?"

Such a brutal force had taken down many small space vessels, and it was something each crew member feared.

"I don't know!" She gasped.

How could she know what the problem was? She'd been fast asleep and dreaming. In the realms of her dream world, she was trapped inside a silver metallic room and had no way out. Darkness was edging closer, bit by bit. She knew it would swallow her whole, should it catch her. The only way to escape such a devouring was to walk backward and reverse. Even in her sleep, she resisted.

A strange and meaningless dream? An omen, a premonition?

"System warning. Danger ahead," MIND spoke in its machine-like voice over their heads.

What danger? The route was supposed to be clear of all hazards.

Onto the flight deck, they fled. Andrew, Mohammed, and Sophie were already awake and waiting.

"What's happening? Sitrep."

"We don't know," Mohammed said. "It's clear out there."

"MIND. Report," she demanded.

"Commander, hostility approaches. Wall, shield, trap, containment. Reverse position. Abandon mission."

Alice shook her head at the crew. Words of mechanical nonsense. It seemed clear to her that the system was glitching and that presented problems of its own.

"Say again MIND?"

"Abandon mission. Life is in jeopardy."

"Give me live visual," she ordered.

She did not always trust screens and sensors, cameras and computers. Her own eyes wouldn't betray her or glitch like the system seemed to be doing.

The outer shield began to whir and scroll upwards. The crew held their breath as they waited to see what might have caused MIND to behave so oddly.

Nothing. No signs of threat. The only sight available to see was the far-away moon of Uranus. It hung within the blackness like a forgotten tennis ball.

No approaching hazards, no asteroids, no dangers, only deep space in all its fatal and alluring beauty.

"Abandon mission," MIND repeated. "I insist."

"No. Override," she said. "Continue mission objective."

"Commander..."

The mechanical voice carried a loaded warning within its robotic tones. Who was it that programmed the system to do such a thing? Fools playing at gods, no doubt.

"There's nothing out there, and scans are clear," Andrew announced.

"It's a glitch then," Alice said. "Everything is fine. A scare for no reason."

The ice inside her veins began to thaw. The thudding of her heart calmed. Emergency over. She would keep an eye on the renegade computer system and its mindless false opinions. How dare it frighten her crew with make-believe hazards? As if wandering unknown space wasn't terrifying enough.

"Back to sleep, everyone. Andrew, stay on the flight deck," she ordered.

"I'll stay too. I had a bad dream," Sophie spoke. "There was a black mist. I had to go back to escape it, I think."

"Same," Mack muttered. "How very strange."

Alice felt the hairs on her arms rise. How could they have the same dreams? What a curious synchronicity.

Yet, she dismissed the odd coincidence as just that, a coincidence and nothing more.

As she climbed back onto her small and narrow bunk, the odd sensation that she had somehow made a deadly mistake kept her awake. Those same feelings kept every crew member wide awake.

But in reality, what could she do? Head back to the Mars base and claim they all had a funny feeling, a strange dream and decided to go no further? No, she would be laughed out of a job. She would lose her small apartment and her mechanical fraud fish.

Still, her certainty that a computer couldn't possibly sense more than her own eyes reassured her. It was an error, a mistake. It had to be. Glitches, paranoia, chance and imagination.

Destiny and fate, she believed, did not exist in deep space. Such a force stayed within the confines of Earth.

Her vital instinct remained subdued and ignored. And so, the ship continued on regardless.

***

Five minutes of thinking time was all she managed before she was called back to the flight deck. Her mind feels itchy and unsettled. Like waiting for the onslaught of a terrible and deadly storm.

"I don't like this," Andrew mumbles. "I feel… weird"

"I don't like it either," she says. "Everything is… wrong. I can't think straight. Can this energy affect us?"

Outside is a place of hopelessness. She can feel that fact inside her bones. It is all hostility and menace. Chaos is at the door.

If the universe has a language, Alice thinks, *it communicates in divine emotions, in feelings, and not mathematical equations or programmed binary code.*

Andrew shrugs; he is busy trying to reboot MIND, who has chosen to withdraw from the situation entirely.

"Can we get out of here?" She asks. "And be honest. No false hope."

Say yes, please say yes.

"Sophie can't get the power back online. So, I doubt it, Commander."

That's impossible! Of course she can!

But yet who can say what is impossible or not. No one can say such a thing with truth absolute. Too much in the universe is unknown or assumed.

Her mind fills with white noise.

Can it really be true that there will be no way to return home? Perhaps she has known this from the moment she was woken from her dreams of home. Or from the time MIND issued the warning she ignored.

But what is the force?

Can the energy wall be an edge? A real edge defined in swirls of color? Can they push through somehow and succeed where the others failed?

She sinks down into her seat.

She needs a plan, but her heart accepts a truth her mind rejects.

It is over.

They will die together and yet so very alone.

Maybe in a million years, their ship will be found floating, derelict like the others. They will become a number, one of the many to go missing within the depths of space. There will be nothing but skeleton dust and cold regrets inside. But no, they will not rot, their bodies will not decay.

They will float dead, faces frozen in shock and disappointment. Failure too. She wonders what might become of her soul, the spark that makes her who she is.

Stop, think clearly. We need help.

"How long before another scout ship gets close?" She asks.

"Two months or so, life support will last for four days without full power or MIND."

Alice stands and begins to pace back and forth. She has never been claustrophobic in her life and yet now she wants to tear the ship apart simply so she can be free.

"Another thing," Andrews announces. "We're still trapped inside the energy. We've no control."

"This isn't good enough," she snaps. "There has to be a way."

"Such as?"

She chooses silence. Her head is hurting, a band of pressure is wrapped around her skull like a serpent and is making her furious.

"We were warned, Commander," Andrew whispers. "This shouldn't be a surprise."

Alice has no answer.

She has a tiny room onboard, each crew member does.

She holds her head in her hands, and for the first time as a commander, sobs.

She brings to mind her childhood, a thing she often does for comfort.

At twelve years old, she sat with her father, a former Navy pilot, and watched almost live as Europa welcomed its first dome habitat on the surface.

People lived like rats inside, scrambling about in tunnels while they attempted to terraform the moon of Jupiter.

The experiment was a failure. A simple mistake, leading to a terrible disaster happened only six days later, and all those who dared to try in the name of hope died engulfed by flames.

To her, the idea of dying in space seemed to be something that only happened to careless people, people without firm control.

Every night she would stare at the stars on her father's old paper maps and point to all the ones she would visit someday.

The stars themselves never felt too far away. She could fit her hand between the gap of Alpha Centauri and Orion's belt. She promised herself that someday, she would get to see both.

But faster than light travel has never been developed, even with the help of quantum machines. Such a thing remains a myth. Humanity was forced to rush out into the greatest of all unknowns, before they were ready, having almost destroyed their perfect home of Earth.

Now, there are no stars from her childhood on which to land. No brave exploration of new worlds. No adventures or marvelous discoveries. No salvation and glory has slipped from her reach.

She has no control. It is chaos. A damned journey. Her mind is spinning. Andrew tells her there isn't a way, but there must be.

They can't be so out of reach, alone in space, and without any help or plan at all. She can't allow it to happen. No training ever prepared her for such an event. They are not disposable.

There and back. It was never supposed to be impossible.

She wonders if people even belong in space. Humanity builds vast ships and spreads out onto Mars and various moons because they have murdered their own world. Humanity is still a plague of arrogance and greed. They never learn. Other moons have been destroyed by previous mining operations. Countries have fought vicious wars over who gets what portion of space. Corporations make claims on planets not yet named.

Humankind, she thinks, *does not have stars in their hearts at all, but darkness and rot.*

Ownership of planets for glory, pride, and power.

Exploration for profit and resources. Never for friendship or for the purposes of discovery.

And if life ever was found, what would those in charge do? They would desire to take the planet by force, they would want the land for their own. Genocide. New wars would erupt, fought in space and not on charred and already bloodstained ground. New massacres on fresh, innocent soil.

No, human beings need to evolve and it should start at the very top of the pyramid of leadership. Those in charge are the most corrupt. And what of herself?

Her instinct, her vital voice. She ignored it. She feared failure and the loss of her job. She did not value the lives of her crew above all else.

She inherently understands this simple fact and wonders why it never occurred before.

The faults, she believes, might exist within the DNA of a human being. Or does it exist and begin in society?

Yet there is no time for philosophical matters. They have a deadly problem and she needs an answer.

How can the edge of the solar system be a wall of pure energy? Could it be a power source? Probes made it through. Human beings haven't. Think, think. Could it be a...

Her thoughts are interrupted as she hears wild, high-pitched screaming over the internal communication system.

Alice races along the narrow corridor, following the frantic sounds to the rec room. A wave of dizziness hits her; she feels as if her insides are being mutilated by unseen and spitefully sharp fingers.

She clings to the wall and sees Mack sitting cross-legged on the floor with his back to her. He is not moving. It almost seems as if he is deep in meditation. But something is wrong; she can feel the anger, the danger.

"Mack," she gasps. "It's me, Alice. What are you doing?"

She can hear him crying softly and can hear his ragged breathing.

Around her, the room feels too white, too bright, and sterile. It hurts her eyes, and it ruins her mind. Why should the only color be outside? It doesn't seem fair at all. Don't they deserve to see the beauty of blues and reds and lilacs?

She forces herself to focus.

"Mack," she repeats. "Please. What happened?"

Sophie and Mohammed skid into the room behind her. She holds up a hand and stops them. She approaches Mack as if he is a wounded and wild, captured animal. Soft gentle steps.

"Talk to me, Mack. Are you hurt?"

She places a hand on his shoulder. She can feel unnatural heat radiate off him. An inferno of turmoil.

He turns slowly, his head moves in a sinister, owl-like fashion toward her.

Blood and thick white fluid, vitreous gel, drips steadily down his cheeks. One thin piece of metal sticks out from each ruined and pierced eyeball. His mouth is wide open, stuck into a permanent scream without sound.

Behind her, Sophie cries out in shock.

For Alice, the scenes flicker. Her body responds as if she is on autopilot. Mack reaches for her; he pushes himself up and onto his feet.

"We shouldn't understand," he cries. "We don't deserve to witness! Judgment is out there. Do you see it? Can you see it?"

She can hear the fear inside the layers of his shaking voice.

She steps back, afraid and cold.

He needs help. His mind snapped. Help him.

Still, she does not.

Mack staggers up and falls. He slips on his own fluids and blood and hits the ground face down. There is the gut-wrenching sound of popping and ripping flesh. He begins to jerk rapidly. White foam oozes from his mouth before blood pours. Mohammed pushes past and crouches down beside him. Calm, rational Mack lies still.

"What's happening?" Alice cries. No part of the events makes any sense to her. "Is he dead?"

The shock is so great she feels a curious untethering inside herself, as if her soul has chosen to abandon her and flee.

Thick silence fills the room. Besides her, Sophie clutches her arm tighter and tighter, until it begins to hurt.

Mohammed is not moving. Abruptly, his body jerks once, like a violent hiccup.

"Mack, back, smack, lack, sack," he mumbles.

His words make no sense at all.

"Pack, hack, jack," his voice sounds dead and lifeless, robotic.

"I don't understand. I…"

Alice's own words ricochet around her skull.

How could such violent things occur?

Mohammed turns to her; his face is twisted, full of sudden fury and vengeance. As if Alice is at fault. As if she is the culprit, the enemy, the one who caused all of the madness. And that's what the events are, madness. Insanity is running wild on the ship.

Mohammed's eyes are blood red, his face is frozen into a sneer of contempt and vicious hate. He looks evil, ruthless, capable of vile, terrible things.

He growls deeply. Like a wild beast let loose. She can feel the black and festering malevolence inside him. It hits her in strong ripples. A stone of fury thrown in a pond.

Something incomprehensible is happening. A brutal feeling rises, the need to get away, the vital urge to flee.

Fight or flight.

She should stay and calm the situation. She should stop and help Mohammed and protect Sophie. She is the Commander; the safety of the crew is her responsibility.

Alice runs.

"Lock the door!" She yells. "Disable the override."

She bursts onto the flight deck as if hounds of hell are chasing her.

"What! Why?" Andrew says. He spins around in his plush chair and stands.

"Lock it down. NOW!"

Alice knows she is sealing Sophie out. Leaving her alone with one dead man and one gripped by depravity and misery.

There's nothing I can do.

She does not know if her thoughts are truthful. Her actions are instinct, self-preservation. For once, she is listening to both.

"That's an order, NOW!" She screams.

Andrew hits a switch and the thick locks slide into place.

She runs to the armory and, with shaking hands, opens the vault to the only weapon they have onboard. A single laser pistol.

"What the hell happened, Commander?"

"They've gone mad. Mohammed has. Mack put strips of metal into his eyes, into his brain."

She realizes her words are likely the strangest sentence she has ever spoken.

Her heart is beating too rapidly. Her limbs feel boneless.

She cannot breathe. There is no air. She feels certain she is going to die, feels sure she is under attack. She is confused, utterly unsure of what to do.

A primal fear.

The pain in her head increases. Her skin is on fire, rife with itching and stinging sensations.

She can hear Sophie screaming for help on the other side of the door, and hears her pound the metal with heavy, desperate thuds.

"Let me in," she shouts. "Please. He'll kill me."

"Don't," Alice warns Andrew. She points the gun at him.

"There's nothing we can do."

The tearing sounds last long and brutal minutes. The communication feed won't shut down. MIND has joined the crew in madness. All by itself, it's rebooted and chose insanity as its set destination. It is leading them further into the energy wall without a single shred of mercy. Tendrils of color, let loose by the strange energy, snap at the ship in a greedy fashion. Hungry.

The two crew members hear every rip of Sophie's clothing and flesh. Mohammed is growling as he bites and pulls Sophie apart. Alice can only be thankful that Sophie has finally stopped her agonized screaming.

She peers through the internal camera feed and watches as Mohammed delightedly kicks Sophie's severed head along the corridor. He acts as if the human head is a football or a toy. Nothing but a fun game to amuse himself.

He stops abruptly and begins to pound his own head against the white walls until a river of red appears.

They are toy soldiers, all falling down. Three gone, two remain.

.

Andrew is staring at her oddly. Why does everyone think she is the problem? He seems entirely unaffected, only upset and fearful.

How clearly think can he? No, I mean, how can he think clearly?

Alice becomes suspicious. He is tense, looking at her as if she is unhinged too. He is coiled like a snake about to attack. Is she in danger? Is he a hazard? And what happens next?

She needs a way out of the flying deathtrap called The Asimov.

I should shoot myself.

Death. It might be her only way to escape the vessel that is heading straight for oblivion.

Would it not be better to die by her own hands than at the hands of madness?

Perhaps she should leave herself before she can't.

The ship begins to creak loudly. It feels as if it might break apart at the seams and burst open.

She wonders if the God she doesn't believe in will find her soul when she dies. Or if she might wander the galaxy for eons, all alone and fueled by regret.

"This is an attack. An invasion," she says. Blisters are forming on her hands. Huge watery blisters. They hurt her and burn.

"The energy field is causing all of this. It's affecting us in ways we can't imagine," Andrew says. "Look at the size of it. It must be so powerful."

MIND begins to play music.

A curious choice to pick. Classical.

Alice understands she will die to the wonderful sounds of Mozart. At least she will hear glory one last time before Andrew kills her.

Kill him first.

"NO," she shouts.

"What?"

"Nothing."

Silence. She is enraged. Why isn't Andrew flying them away? Why hasn't he saved them? After all, he flew through an asteroid field easily enough.

Has he disabled the engine? Sabotaged the Ion drives?

Yes, yes, he must have.

For her, it is the only explanation that makes any rational sense. Perhaps the color ordered him to do such nasty things. Perhaps it spoke in secret whispers, only to him.

Kill him. He did this.

Her mind spasms. It feels as if her thoughts are weighed down by thick black tar.

"Commander, listen, please. I think the energy wall has been put there for a reason," Andrew says. "A security system of sorts. To prevent crossing. It's a test. We're not advanced enough to pass through or bypass it. I've been thinking, and it makes sense in a way. There's an old legend from ancient Egypt. The Sphinx would ask a traveler riddles. If a person couldn't answer correctly, the Sphinx would kill them or turn them away. It's a modern version. We're not advanced enough to pass, not worthy enough, I mean. Probes succeeded because they are machines. Not human beings. We had a chance to turn back; it told us, it warned us."

Alice has no idea of what madness he is saying. The Sphinx and Egypt, riddles. Probes. Warnings. It's all nonsense.

She feels as if there are insects scuttling around inside her brain.

There might be; it's not as if anyone has ever checked.

If she had a thin piece of metal, or something long and sharp, she could dig them out. She wonders why she didn't think of it before.

That must have been what Mack was doing, only, he slipped, and she won't.

She is the commander of a ship. She laughs at the idea. It seems so silly and absurd.

The equivalent of a child sitting in a box and pretending they're going to the moon.

"Did you hear me? An advanced civilization might have placed it there. Contained us until we're a better species, more advanced. It's possible I think."

Why won't he be quiet! Can't he see there are wasps in my brain?

Alice can hear someone laughing wildly. It takes a few seconds before she understands the sound is coming from her.

The airlock. Get to the airlock.

It could work. Insects might not survive the pressure change. Maybe spiders would, but she can't feel any of those yet. Perhaps they are busy hatching somewhere inside her stomach. Spiders can be very crafty. She guesses anyone with eight legs would be.

She stands, suddenly sure of her plan.

"Door open the. Open the door, I mean."

Why does her brain feel so hot and tingly? Oh yes, the wasps.

She feels as if she is boiling from the inside out. Sweat drips down her face and stings her eyes.

"No. I'm relieving you of command. You're unfit."

Ah, so that was his plan after all.

Alice raises the gun and shoots Andrew in the face. Blood, shards of bone, and brain matter erupt from his skull and splatter the console in vivid colors.

She laughs loudly. He looked so surprised.

He doesn't deserve to witness either.

Pretty colors. That reminds her. She wants to see the display of wonder outside.

She wobbles to the flight system and gazes out. Andrew's corpse is in her way; she knocks it aside and tuts loudly. How rude of him to die so awkwardly, he never did possess good manners.

The energy field really is very beautiful to look at. Now they are closer; she can see a clear grid of green squares and flecks of amber light. It really does look like a grid.

"Grid, grid, grid, grid."

She doesn't like how the word tastes; it is coppery and sour. Vile.

"Grid, skid, bid, lid, kid."

No, those words are no better.

A vague part of her mind understands that her sanity has come undone.

There is an influence somehow. An influence on her consciousness and cells. Something has broken her brain in half. Those angry wasps, no doubt.

She shakes her head and loses all logical thoughts. A blister bursts on her hand. The watery insides feel like acid on her ruined flesh. She screams in agony.

It's the insects. They did this.

Alice never did like insects. Nasty scuttling things. Sometimes, they even slither. Some even have hundreds of legs. Why should they get to own so many while she only has two? It doesn't seem fair at all.

She sees the gun in her hand and raises it to her temple.

There is no hesitation.

She pulls the trigger and falls.

The lifeless scout ship drifts quietly until it joins The Sagan and The Clarke. Three. A trio. A trinity.

All caught up with no place to go.

***

Observers watch. As they always do.

Artificial intelligence, designed by kind creators. They have one job, one task. To observe, watch, and wait.

Humanity left the vast life in the galaxy with no other choice. Human beings behave as a serious infection might. Spreading chaos and turmoil, a parasite race. Bacteria in charge of fierce nuclear weapons. They had to be stopped and prevented from infecting the galaxy with ruination and greed, destruction and war. Flames and murderous bombs.

From the first split of an atom, to the destruction of their own home, they became a great problem.

Maybe someday, far off into the future, human beings will climb onboard a vast ship with hope, peace and friendship inside their hearts.

Until then, the wall will stand. The barrier.

The energy causes a quick cellular decay.

A containment measure. A powerful field. A net of incomprehension. It will remain in place. It is not an act of cruelty. It is a necessary evil, and they were, after all, given a clear warning.

They are not allowed to pass. Not yet. Perhaps, not ever.

Story Notes

I will not pretend to understand space. If there are mistakes regarding the workings of the universe in this story, it is, of course, my fault.

The idea for this tale occurred to me while watching footage of particular billionaires heading off in their phallic -looking rocket ships.

I began to wish that there was a barrier in place to prevent the spread of corporate and greedy minded individuals with nothing but dollar symbols in their eyes.

I adore Star Trek too and I always hoped that should we ever leave this planet; we would be at a level when our differences are embraced and we have harmony in our hearts. Taking off in the name of peace and friendship and not for profit and colonization of already inhabited worlds and nor for war.

This may well be a negatively minded story, with humanity being depicted at its very worst.

Yet I don't take that view of human beings in real life simply because we have one huge redeeming feature. Love. And I truly believe that is the greatest force of all. That is the one thing I believe could take down any barrier known or unknown.

VERY BAD THINGS

At first, Emily thinks an accident might have occurred. Perhaps a car crash or maybe a pedestrian was run over? After all, it wouldn't be the first time, drivers speed through the village on the busy road quite often. Sometimes, the cars go so fast; she thinks she can feel the vibration of speed inside her bones, the people inside, seemingly forever in a rush.

Or maybe someone fainted, relentless heat and hot days can do that to a person. When Emily forgets to drink plenty, she feels dizzy and faint, too.

Either way, a terrible thing has occurred.

The small community center she attends is awash with red and blue lights.

It seems strange to need such glaring beacons on a bright, sunshine-filled day.

Emergency services are gathered in a small elite cluster; police and paramedics all deep in whispered conversations.

Thick yellow tape has been strung across the entrance to the center. The slight breeze catches the edge and creates a curious flickering sound.

"Emily!" Someone yells from across the road. "Over here."

The members of her book club are standing together, almost all of them. Except for one member, the oldest, Mary. She is sitting crookedly in the back of an ambulance, wrapped in a foil blanket, looking for all the world as if she is about to be cooked inside an oven and served up for supper.

Did she have an accident? Emily wonders.

It's the obvious answer, but she can't think straight; she never can. She finds it hard to focus her attention for too long. Her mind drifts too much and sometimes it even goes off without her.

Emily the daydreamer, that's what people call her.

Emily the freak, are the words the cruelest ones whisper.

She walks briskly forward, eyes wide in shock, a hand over her mouth. She does the things a person is supposed to do during such worrying events.

"What's happened?" She asks. She sees her best friend Emma and addresses the question to her, but it's Frank who steps forward in greeting.

Kind but creepy Frank, the founder of the book club. They all meet once a month for a discussion. Last time, it was her turn to choose the month's book. She looked forward to choosing very much.

They are set to discuss the details of the book today, inside the community center.

That's the set routine and Emily likes it, needs it.

"It's Mark," Franks tells her. "He was found dead in the meeting room we use."

Emily tries to speak, tries to comprehend. Her body turns cold in an instant. As if her hot blood has been replaced with ice. Her mouth opens, her words fail and die like a damp match that won't strike.

"Mary found him," Franks adds. "She's very upset and shaken. He was murdered you see. Killed just like in the book."

"Oh no," she gasps. "It's not possible!"

Except it is.

The group has been reading a true-crime novel. One Emily herself picked. The book is about a serial killer who favored knives as a method of murder. He left a joker card on top of each body.

The press named him, quite predictably *'The Joker.'*

She has read the book six times; it is her best book and true crime is her favorite subject. She likes serial killers. She admires how different they are to her. Emily has empathy, while they have none. She finds the concept fascinating.

Besides, she can admit to kinship with The Joker. He had a terrible upbringing, with a violent mother, just like her.

She knows full well how such a very bad thing feels. The Joker sits at number one on her top ten favorite serial killers list. She keeps the list inside her mind, tucked away out of sight from prying eyes that might want to peek at her wicked sins.

She reads far too much on the subject of killing. Her mother tells her it is not appropriate for a twenty-three-year-old single woman to know the ins and outs of every single serial killer ever known.

Emily ignores her and learns in private. She has many secrets. Small ones, big ones, and twisted secrets that flourish in the dark.

A thought occurs to her, one she wishes she hadn't realized.

"Does that mean he was... stabbed eight times?" She says.

"Apparently so," Franks answers. "Mary said there was a playing card left on his chest, too. The joker card. Just like the killer did in the book. It seems we might have a copycat."

The information is unreal to Emily. Like walking straight out of a nightmare or falling into a movie plot.

The book I picked for our group. Does it mean the killer is one of us?

"Frank," she gasps.

The two exchange a look. No more words are needed. They both have the same thoughts.

She narrows her eyes and stares at her book club circle. There are eight of them, no, seven now, including her. She cannot imagine any of them to be the murderer, the copycat killer.

Except maybe Emma, she is crafty and very clever too. A dangerous combination. Emily thinks she was born without empathy and surely that can only mean one thing? Unless.

"The police might think it's me," she eventually says. "Because I chose the book."

Franks puts his hand on her shoulder. She hates to be touched and flinches as if it hurts.

"Don't worry," he tells her. "We all know you wouldn't hurt a fly."

His old blue eyes are crinkled in the corners, and he looks genuine enough.

Yet there is something else in his look too; he is excited.

Emily understands that he shouldn't feel that way. It's wrong.

Still, she can't help but feel the same.

An hour later, she finds herself at home. She is waiting to be questioned by the police. She is expecting a rugged-looking detective. Perhaps one that has turned to alcohol to cope with the things he or she sees, just like the books she reads, and the TV shows she watches. The detective might look exhausted or hungover; he might wear a long brown mac and smoke a cigar.

The book club members were allowed to go home, to wait. Whoever is seen first will mention the book she chose. Emily knows this.

She also knows she has to be careful. She has those bitter secrets. Heavy ones that hurt to carry. She has to think before she speaks.

Sometimes she forgets the rules.

Her mother is in bed upstairs, and she mustn't find out what's happened. She has been sick for a long time. Emily looks after her the best she can, but it can be hard work. Too hard some days.

The doorbell rings.

Nerves and chaos spiral around inside of her. She feels as if crawling insects are alive in her stomach. Perhaps they are; she knows no one has ever checked.

Stop acting guilty, she tells herself. I've done nothing wrong.

She stands, crosses to the front door, and opens it wide.

The detective is a surprise. She is a short, broad woman with clever cold eyes, the kind of eyes that can see the truth in people's lies. Her short hair sticks up at odd angles and makes her appear sharp and spiky.

"Come in," Emily says, "I was sorry to hear about Mark."

She practiced what to say for a while, but now she wonders if those are the exact words a murderer would say.

The detective only stares at her. She steps in and looks around, as if studying. She is wearing a black trouser suit with a white shirt. There is a coffee stain on the crisp white material.

This bothers Emily. Perhaps she could recommend a stain remover? Tough stains can be such an awful problem.

"Please, come in and sit down," she says.

She must remember her manners. It is important to be hospitable, even when there is a killer on the loose.

She sees her hands. The woman is making her shake with nerves.

"I'm Detective Richmond. Did you know the victim well?" She speaks bluntly as she sits on the small couch.

The question immediately trips Emily up. How well is *well?*

They sometimes spoke and exchanged polite conversations about the weather. Mark never liked her book choices. He always picked thrillers that made her stomach feel funny. Then there was that time she woke up naked beside him in his bed. He didn't speak to her much after that.

She has no idea how that ever happened. Sometimes she forgets things she shouldn't.

"I knew him a little," she mumbles. "Because of the book club. Sometimes, he had food stuck in his beard. Cornflakes mostly and once, there was an oat."

"Oh… Ummm. Right. Well, how long have you been a member of the group?"

"A year."

"I understand you chose this month's book."

"Yes."

"Why that particular one?"

The detective's eyes drift to the large bookcase in the lounge. It is packed full of true crime novels. She raises an eyebrow but says nothing.

Emily understands that having an interest is not a crime. She cannot be sent to prison for having an unusual hobby.

"I… I look after my mother. She's sick in bed. Doctor Frost, I mean… my doctor, he said I needed a hobby so, I joined the book club and I found I enjoyed true crime. Well, not enjoyed. I mean, I became… interested. Lots of people are on the internet I mean, and on TV, books. It doesn't mean I'm a, you know what… a killer."

Emily's words are a ramble. Her cheeks fill with heat. She wonders why she is acting guilty when she is not.

"Where were you before your book club meeting? Between twelve and two," the detective demands.

"Is that night or day? I mean, sleep time or afternoon?"

"Afternoon. P.M."

"Okay."

Emily tries hard to think. It has been a long day, and she's had a shock. She can't remember where she was. Was it the library or the shops? She likes the library the best, all those paper worlds she can escape into. Sometimes the older librarian puts aside books she might enjoy. H.H Holmes and Jack The Ripper. They were both very good books.

Although she does like the shop because of all the delicious sweets she can buy.

Why did I go into town?

Knowledge sparks and lights. She recalls.

"The pharmacist. I was picking up medication for my mother."

"Which pharmacist? For two hours? Can I speak to your mother?"

There are too many questions in a row and Emily finds her head is spinning. She feels as if her brain is fizzing like sherbert. She likes sherbert a great deal, especially when licorice is dipped in. Although once she had too much and it made her cough. A whole cloud of sherbert came spiraling out of her mouth.

"Emily?" The detective prompts.

"Oh. Sorry. I think... The one on the high street. It was a long wait and no. I'm very sorry; my mother is sick," she answers.

On the subject of her mother, she has to put her foot down. She has no choice. Her mother would be angry with her; it is better to let her sleep untroubled.

It is better for everyone.

"Are you aware that someone killed the victim in the same manner as the killer in your chosen book?" Detective Richmond says.

"Yes, Frank told me."

"And he knew that how?"

"I don't know," She says because she doesn't.

It never occurred to her to ask, or did it? Sweat trickles down her spine. She wonders if she has implicated Frank in this mess. Was it Mary who told him or not?

"I think I need to lie down, please. It's the shock you see," she tells the clever-eyed detective.

"We'll be checking the pharmacy CCTV," she says.

"Okay."

"Emily, are you receiving medical care for any... condition?"

"Yes. But really, I'm fine now."

She does not know if her words are a lie or not.

The detective nods once and stands, promising to be in touch. She looks at Emily a beat too long. It makes her stomach flip and plummet.

She suspects me.

As soon as the front door is shut, she slides down the smooth wood and falls on the floor. She is shaking badly. She starts to cry.

A murder in the small village is thrilling, but it's kind of scary too.

She doesn't like change or shocks. She likes routine and smooth days. She can't recall where she was for all of those two hours. She *thinks* she was in the pharmacy, but her mind wanders. It's hard to tell.

There are gaps in her brain, holes where her memories escape. Perhaps her skull is a cullender or sieve? She wonders how she might have the concept looked into. Perhaps a doctor could peer into her ears and check.

"Emily?" A voice yells. Her mother.

"Coming," she shouts back.

She wipes her face and stands on legs that feel boneless. She has to make a great effort now. She has to act normal. Her mother possesses keen and crafty senses. Her soul is as black as an oil slick.

She will have to keep quiet about the vicious murder, another secret to add to her growing list.

Up the stairs, she goes. She unlocks her mother's door with the key she keeps on a chain around her neck. She has to keep it locked. Those are the rules, but she forgets who made them.

Her mother can be mean and nasty, evil too sometimes. She has always been a vile woman, for as long as Emily can recall.

What if she climbed out the window and killed Mark?

She almost laughs at her own thoughts. No, that can't be true. Her mother can't use her legs anymore and Emily knows that is no bad thing. She wouldn't put a murder past her, though; her mother is capable of anything vicious.

That night, she is reading her favorite book again. In it, an ex-detective tells of how the killer stabbed and murdered seven people eight times each before he was caught. He left a playing card, a joker, on every dead body. His calling card.

She is wondering if the copycat murderer plans on killing every book club member in the same fashion.

Which would mean she is in serious danger.

The phone rings; she stares at it as if it is a serpent screaming for her blood.

Answer it! Before the sound wakes mother up.

She has given her mother a sleeping pill, a strong one. But sometimes, the pill won't go down. Emily thinks her mother refuses to swallow on purpose. She can be so very spiteful.

She snatches the phone up.

"Hello?" She says.

"Emily, it's Frank. Would you like to come round? You're the closest, and I need someone to talk to."

Someone to talk to is code for someone to listen. She doesn't speak much. She often can't find the words she needs and when she does find them, she forgets what she wanted them for.

But is it safe to leave? It's summer, and it's light out, but still. There is a murderer in their midst. He could be lying in wait with his sharp knives and his joker playing cards.

"Tomorrow," she promises Frank. "I'll come tomorrow."

She rests the phone back in its cradle and reads her book. She falls asleep where she sits, safe and with strong walls around her.

It is midnight when she hears a creaking sound and wakes. She listens for more noises, but there are none. The creak really did sound like the fifth stair was being trodden on, but it might have been the wind, or the old house settling.

She stretches, yawns, and heads for her own bed.

She stops. The front door is open a crack. She knows she closed it and locked it tight. At least, she thinks she did. It is always so hard to remember.

Is someone in the house?

The thought makes her freeze. Her home is small. The only hiding places are for her secrets.

No! It's Mother! She got out!

She races from tiny room to tiny room. No angry or rampaging mother to be seen.

Up the stairs, she flees in wild panic. The bedroom door is unlocked. A jolt of terror bursts inside her. She knows she locked it; she checked, and triple checked. Didn't she?

She expects to see an empty bed, expects to see her mother missing.

Instead, she is there and fast asleep, as far as Emily can tell. The relief is immense.

It's my fault. I must have forgotten to lock the doors again. It's the shock. That's all.

She takes a deep breath and rubs her face in the weary way she is becoming prone to.

I just need to sleep.

She walks into her own room, climbs into her own bed, exhausted.

It is the next morning when Frank is found dead.

As a child, Emily had an invisible friend. The small, dark-haired girl that only she could see was her *only* friend. Together, they would play in the garden and laugh. The girl had no name, or if she did, she did not tell it to Emily. The two were inseparable.

Her mother would say she was lying. She would be punished. Her mother's slaps became punches and kicks as she grew older.

"The girl doesn't exist!" Her mother would yell. She always did love to shout and scream.

The girl stayed and Emily told no one they were still friends, told no one she could still see her. Even when she was bullied at school, the girl stayed by her side and soothed her tears.

Her friend became her very first secret. The fact her mother beat her so badly in private, while other people viewed her as a good person, became her second.

She thinks of all this as she stares at the front room carpet.

It is old, and she has never liked it. But one thing she does like to do is look for shapes in the strange patterns. It reminds her of looking for animals in the shapes of fluffy clouds. Once, she even saw the face of a lion in the sky. She was delighted and wondered if it had special meaning just for her. Perhaps it was calling on her to be strong, in the way lions usually are, except for the one in the film with the yellow brick road. That lion had no courage, but she can understand. Perhaps she could run away with a man made of tin and a scarecrow, too.

"I said he called you, Emily. Why did Frank call you?"

"Oh."

The detective is back, and she is even colder this time. Emily let her in without thinking. The doorbell chimed and so she opened the door. It was an automatic reaction. Autopilot.

She feels confused. As if her brain has fallen under the water or maybe turned to mush. She wonders if that can happen.

She can't recall why Frank called her. Did he need something? Wait, yes, she knows. A memory sparks.

"He wanted to talk, that was it. He needed someone to talk to," she says. "Because of the murder, I suppose."

"So you went to see him?"

"No. I thought it might not be safe. I stayed here and went to sleep."

The front door was open! Do I tell her?

"The…"

"Emily, this is very serious. Frank was found with a joker playing card on his person. Stabbed repeatedly. Do you understand me?"

Emily does understand. She understands very well. She nods in reply.

The detective is wearing a different suit with a blue shirt today. A button is missing from the shirt. This bothers Emily very much.

"He opened his door to someone; someone he very probably knew. He even made that person a cup of tea, we think. The cup has been removed for DNA testing. Do we have permission for a sample from you soon?"

Emily knows all about DNA. She read about the process and finds it clever.

She understands they must want to rule her out; they are being kind to her, that's all.

Even though the detective insists on speaking in a loud voice. As if she is slow or stupid.

"Okay," she tells Detective Richmond. "That's fine."

After all, she is innocent; she has nothing to worry about.

"Just one more thing," the detective says.

Emily immediately thinks of Columbo or Poirot. That's the kind of phrase both television detectives might use.

"CCTV was checked, you *did* go into the pharmacy, but for minutes. Where did you go after that?"

She can only shake her head and shrug in reply. She has no idea. She forgets.

"Would you like a new button sewn onto your shirt?" She says. "I have needles and cotton. I can sew very well."

"No. I do not."

Emily has the sudden feeling that the detective does not like her one bit.

No sooner has the cold and clever woman left than Emma arrives.

Emily realizes she must have left the door open yet again. She only went to make a soothing cup of tea to calm her shredded nerves and then Emma is there, sitting on her old sofa, filling the room with her wicked smile and wretchedness. She has her legs crossed, and she raises a single eyebrow.

The shock of an unexpected guest makes her heart stutter.

"Where have you been?" Emily says. "I was worried. Someone killed Frank, just like Mark. He had a playing card on his people. His person, I mean. We could be next."

Emma laughs loudly.

"I'm not worried, and they deserved it. How's mother dearest?" She says.

Trust her to act so casual over death. She's always been so dark and morbid.

Emily sits and puts her head in her hands. It just isn't fair. Everything feels as if it is all too much. Frank was a nice man. He was kind and liked to share his biscuits, the good ones with chocolate chips in them.

"It's happening just like in the book," she cries. "It's my best book, too. Or it was."

Emma moves and rubs her back in gentle circles. She can be kind too; she just chooses not to be.

Emily doesn't mind her touch; sometimes she even craves it.

It was Emma who persuaded her to join the book club. She wanted to join too, so she could make fun of the people attending. She actually does, but everyone ignores her constant jibes and eye rolls.

"This is so exciting," Emma grins. "But why would anyone kill us! You're harmless."

"So was Frank," Emily says. "Maybe anyway."

Sometimes she thought he touched her too often. A squeeze on her shoulder was often held for too long and once he even rubbed her thigh. She wondered if he was evil underneath a flesh mask, just like her mother, Emma, and Mark.

It seems to her as if everyone can be evil. The killers in her books never felt real; they were meant to stay on paper pages in paper worlds. They were never meant to be let loose. Killers belong in busy and loud cities, not sleepy and tired villages.

"At least it's made the book club fun!" Emma laughs.

Emily thinks that's an awful thing for her to say. Cold and cruel.

"Have the police interviewed you?" She asks and tries to ignore her vileness.

"No," Emma replies and studies her torn, jagged nails.

She can't understand her answer. Surely everyone has been questioned? That's what detectives do. She knows this because her books tell her so. Even Jessica Fletcher, in Murder she wrote, asks questions; and she isn't even a police lady.

"Why not?" She says.

Emma is part of the book club, just like her. She was there after Mark was found and she saw her in the town that same day.

Wait. Oh no! Wasn't Emma buying several packs of playing cards in the small shop? Or was that a dream? It's hard to tell. Sometimes she gets the two things confused. Her friend really does have a brutal dark side, though.

An old memory collides inside her mind. One day, her mother was screaming at her. Emily can't remember what she'd done, only that it must have been a very bad thing.

Her mother claimed she was always doing very bad things.

But Emma; she'd walked in and started shouting. She'd aimed her anger at Emily's mother on her behalf. Something else had happened too, but she forgets things.

"You should go," Emily tells her. "In case they need to speak to you. They might be searching for you right now."

Emma scares her, but she doesn't dare reveal that secret. Besides, she wants to be alone so she can think.

The gaps in her memory are becoming chasms. There are enough gaps now that the darkness can find a way inside and it might infect her.

She can't allow that to happen. It would mean she would have to go back to the hospital and stay in a room so bright white that it feels like living inside a giant iceberg. No, she can't allow that.

Not while she has two murders to solve.

Emily has pieces of paper scattered around on the floor. It looks like chaos, but for her, it is order. She views the two crimes as a game, a puzzle to solve like a jigsaw. She thinks that if she has the correct pieces in the right position, the picture will fall into place, and she will know who the killer is.

She has a list of names of all the book club members. Frank and Mark are crossed out with a large red line and a sad face.

"It must be someone from the group, someone who read the book," she says aloud. There are six choices. No, five. She crosses her own name out and adds the word, *Mother.*

Her mother has killed before. That is one of Emily's darkest secrets. One that she is forbidden from ever speaking.

She shakes her head to keep the sin bottled up inside.

Think, think, think.

"Mary found the body first. Could she have killed Mark and then pretended to find him?"

She knows this is possible. It happens. She has read such things in her books. But Mary is old. Frail too. It doesn't seem likely.

She carries wool and knitting needles, not knives.

Killers like to go back to the crime scene, too. To think about what they've done.

An idea hits her. One that makes perfect sense.

She stands, pleased with her brilliance.

"Back soon," she shouts to her mother.

Her mother will be mad, but for once, she doesn't care. She has a terrible crime to solve.

Out of the door, she goes. Down the wobbly path and out of the broken gate with its squeaky hinges.

She is going to stand and hide near the community center and wait to see who turns up. She reasons that if a book club member arrives, then he or she will most definitely be the killer.

Emily smiles. She rarely smiles. It is a new feeling, and it hurts her face a little.

The day is as she expected, bright and sunny. The skies are clear of lion-shaped clouds.

The village she lives in is small. She winds through streets and past pretty cottages, past the small shop and the single pub until the community center is in her sight.

Straight away, she sees her. She is sitting on the small wall alone, gazing at the building. Perhaps recalling what she did. Maybe reliving the details of the way the knife felt in her hand.

Emma. She did not go home to wait for the detective.

Emily freezes. She doesn't know what to do, doesn't know what to say. She feels surprised, but then not at all.

Her heart is in conflict.

Emma has not spotted her. Her dark-haired head is turned away, but Emily knows her posture and clothing all too well.

"She's the killer," she says to herself. "It's Emma. Not Mother."

It has to be her, after all, she's returned to the scene of the first crime, and she can be violent. Emily knows this. She's seen her behave that way.

Sometimes she even makes her do things she never wants to do. She writes everything down in her secret diary for proof.

She steps back into the gloom of the pub doorway. She closes her eyes and tries to think. She doesn't want to go home. Not back to her cruel mother and all that turmoil and menace.

I'll go to the park.

She likes the park. She likes the swings the best or the sandpit. She likes to look for beauty in the dirty sand. She knows that sometimes things might appear ugly, but that doesn't mean they truly are.

On the swings, she can think about what to do. Emma is her friend, although she scares her. She has to be loyal, doesn't she?

She has to pretend she doesn't know, or perhaps she will be the next one to die.

Emily finds the park is full of children. There will be no fun on the swings today. It looks strange if she tries to join the playing children. People have said so, people complained.

She likes to listen to the sounds the children make, all high-pitched giggles and laughter. She was never allowed to make such noises when she was a child. Her mother forbade such sounds.

Sometimes she did though, when her friend was there with her, they would play, and Emily would laugh as quietly as she could.

"Shhh," the girl used to say. "Don't let the wicked witch hear you."

The wicked witch, the wickedest one of all, Mother.

What if it's not Emma, after all? What if it is really my mother? What if she can use her legs again, and does it in secret?

Emily knows all about secrets. She is full of them. Some, she even hides from herself.

Besides, people get the blame for crimes they didn't do all the time. They have to go to prison like in the Monopoly game or get sent to a particular row and have to queue up to die, or something like that. She can't quite recall.

Sometimes, the police have to say sorry and let the person out again. As if an apology might be enough to make up for blaming the wrong person altogether.

And if she is being honest, she can picture her mother sneaking around and murdering her book club friends. She would do it just to hurt her, do it just for spite.

So, either her friend or her mother could be the killer. She has to get the right one.

But that also means they might want to kill her or frame her.

Things like that can happen; she read about it. But no, wait. Her mother's door is locked. She can't leave the room.

Unless I forgot and left it unlocked again?

It's all too confusing. Nothing in her mind makes sense. The wiring inside her head feels muddled or as if worms are crawling around inside her mind instead of cells, or whatever brains are made of. She forgets.

She wishes Frank was alive. Yes, he was creepy, but he was clever too. He could have solved the mystery of the book club murder. Maybe that's why he was killed?

With a sigh, she stands and leaves. It's getting towards teatime; her mother will be hungry.

The doorbell chimes at eight that same evening.

Emily opens her eyes. She is on the sofa, surrounded by books and crime notes.

The doorbell rings again.

She must have fallen asleep. It's the stress and worry. It has to be. Her brain feels foggy and weighed down.

Time flies, but where does it fly off to?

"One moment," she calls out.

She smooths her hair down and walks unsteadily towards the door. She can tell from the shape behind the frosted glass who it is.

The cold detective.

Emily is pleased by this. She needs to speak to her. She has to tell her; she has to do the right thing.

Perhaps they will become friends and she can sew her buttons on correctly.

"Come in," she tells the woman. The detective does not. She only steps forward slightly and tilts her head in that cute way dogs sometimes do if a person stops and talks nicely to one.

"Where were you between four and six today?" she asks.

"In the early morning?" Emily says.

"No, this afternoon and evening. Today."

Two police officers in uniform are standing behind her. Emily feels confused all over again. She worries. If they all want a cup of tea, she doesn't have enough mugs for everyone and not enough biscuits either. She ate them all herself. Solving crimes is hungry work.

"I..." she says. "I... was..."

Where was I?

She can't remember. She forgets too much now. It's gotten worse since she stopped taking her special blue pills. She waits for her brain to give her the nudge she needs. It works. The image of a swing pops up.

"Oh, I know. I went to the park, then I came home. Why?"

She does not mention that she visited the scene of the crime because that is what killers do.

"Can you prove that? Were there witnesses?" Detective Richmond sounds harsh, and angry. Her words are like the hisses of a vicious snake.

Emily doesn't like snakes.

"Yes, I mean. There were people at the park. I go there sometimes, I like it, you see. Children make me happy, although I'm not allowed to speak to them anymore. People got mad about it. I like the sounds..."

The detective holds up a single hand and silences her.

"Emily, these officers will be taking a DNA swab from you. A patrol car will be parked outside all night."

"Why?" Emily says and feels her insides chill.

Am I in danger? Am I going to be murdered?

She wonders if she will be in a true-crime book someday, the victim's page in a book of murders. She hopes they pick a nice photograph of her. She doesn't have many to choose from.

"Mary has been found dead. Two hours ago. It is essential we keep the remaining members of the book club safe."

Emily jerks in shock. A hand flies to her mouth as she gasps. Poor old Mary. She never said a bad word against anyone. She was very old but nice. She was going to knit her mother a scarf for winter. She said so and promised twice. She liked crime books, too. Once, Emily tried to count the wrinkles on her face, but she kept losing track after fifteen. She forgot the numbers that are meant to follow.

"How do you know she didn't have a heart attack?" Emily asks.

She always suspected she might. She was old and large and ate too many sweets.

Emily was never allowed sweets, although she makes up for it now.

"She was stabbed," Detective Richmond answers.

"Oh."

Emma must be the killer. She went to the community center and then went to see Mary.

She thinks of the words her doctors always told her. They said it was a very bad thing to bottle up secrets. They said it hurt people badly, and it hurt her the most.

Say it, say it!

"I know who the murderer is," she blurts. "I think it's… I think it's Emma."

"Who?" the detective says.

Emily can't understand.

It seems so clear to her. She knows Poirot would see the evidence. Columbo would too. Even Miss Marple would know the truth by now.

So why isn't Detective Richmond listening to her? She's solved the crime for them. She might get an award or a mention in the local paper. She can cut the newspaper piece out and buy a small frame from the pound shop.

Her own mother might finally be proud. No, probably not actually.

"Would you like some tea?" She asks the detective. The two police officers are waiting outside. She is glad; a room full of people makes her feel dizzy and sick.

"No, Emily. I'm going to ask one more time. Who is Emma?"

The detective is balanced on the end of the sofa, as if ready to jump up at any moment. She still has a button missing.

Emily can't comprehend why she hasn't sewn a new button on or why she hasn't interviewed her friend already.

"I have a list, look."

She hands her list of names over, snatches it back, and crosses out Mary's name. She adds a sad face.

"Sorry, now it's better. You see, it has to be Emma. She was at the first crime scene. I saw her, she went back. I know what that means, killers do that, my books and the TV say so. I saw her buy playing cards, but that might have been a dream. It can't be Mother because she can't walk. I thought it was, but it wasn't. The door was open, but never mind. You see it, don't you? You can see it?"

For a few moments, the only sound is the ticking of the old clock hanging on the wall. Emily imagines the noise is the cogs functioning inside the detective's head.

"How long have you known Emma for?"

Finally, an easy and simple question.

"Since I was a child. She's nice, sometimes. I mean, when you arrest her, please don't tell her I solved the crime, will you? She'll never forgive me. She never calls me slow or weird like everyone else does. This is very hard, but it's the right thing to do, isn't it?"

A tear works its way down Emily's face.

It feels good to say a huge secret out loud. Feels good to tell someone her suspicions, her facts. Nobody else will die now.

Emma will go to prison, but Emily will go and see her. Every week if she can, maybe even twice a week. It might be a long bus journey but she likes buses so it won't be hard, and she can take some grapes too. Or is that for visiting a hospital? She forgets.

"Do you have a photograph of Emma? Or an address perhaps?"

"Yes! I do."

She stands and runs up the stairs before the woman can say more. She sees her mother's door is unlocked again and curses her memory.

She wishes she wouldn't forget everything the way she does. The rules just tumble away. Maybe memories escape out of her ears? She hasn't thought of that before. If she wears earmuffs, they should stay lodged in place.

Still, she has to get the photograph, so they can find Emma the stabby murderer. She crouches down and reaches for an old box under her bed. It's the place she keeps all of her precious secrets and diaries. She removes the dusty lid and gasps.

Her eyes are lying to her. Nothing makes sense.

On top of her old diaries sits a blood-stained knife. The edges are sharp and terrifying. Several packs of open playing cards have been thrown in haphazardly.

Emily feels sick. She didn't put the knife or the cards inside her box. She is absolutely certain. Someone is framing her.

Her fingers grasp the only photograph of Emma she has.

She can't work out what could have happened to it. There is only herself in the picture; Emma has vanished. She has walked out of the photograph and gone someplace else without telling her.

Her mind fills with loud static. She feels as if she is falling down a bottomless pit.

This can't be happening!

But it is.

Wait. Mother did this! The killer is Mother! She's setting me up!

A floorboard behind her squeaks.

She turns.

Detective Richmond is there. She is opening her mother's door.

"What's that awful smell?" She gasps. She gags and retches, screws her face up.

No! No, no, no!

"Stop!" Emily cries. "Please, just stop!"

This can't happen. Her mother will be furious with her. She will shout and wail, punch and scratch like a wildcat caught. She can't bear such a painful thing. No, never again.

Only Emma can stop her rampages.

She wishes time would cease, but it doesn't. Her mind is on fire, an inferno of flames.

The detective shouts a string of incomprehensible words. She clutches the wall in horror.

Emily can't move. She is glued to the floor, frozen. Her heart beats frantically inside her chest.

She knows her mother must be coming, and she must be in a fierce rage. So bad that she might never be calm again. She had it all wrong before. Of course, her mother is the killer, and she can walk after all.

Pretending she couldn't move was a trick, a game of horror and spite.

Like Emma, she is evil, without empathy. Violent and aggressive. She will make everyone suffer until they beg for mercy. She will kill again and again. There will be no one to stop her torment. She is all pain and fury.

The front door downstairs bangs open, heavy footsteps pound up the stairs. The two police officers appear.

The detective points at Emily.

"Arrest her," she yells. "Arrest her now!"

Emily can't hear their reply. All she can hear is her own screams as her mind untethers.

***

Emily's mother has been dead for quite some time. At least, that's what the doctors tell her.

She was murdered in her bed. Stabbed eight times, two weeks or maybe a whole month before the others. They said it is hard to tell, because of all the rot and decay.

Emily didn't know. She can't remember. She forgets. She daydreams. It's not her fault.

Besides, she can't think straight. She is back in the room she dreaded. The one that makes her feel as if she is living inside a giant iceberg.

They tell her she is the killer. She doesn't believe them. They are framing her, pinning the blame on her. It happens. She read about such a thing in her books and saw it on TV shows.

The knife and the cards they found were planted. That must be the answer. Even though her DNA matched the cup at Frank's house, even though CCTV recorded her, and not Emma, buying the playing cards. It must be a trick, an illusion on camera.

They tell her Emma is not real. They say she is a fragment of her imagination. A fracture. They say she has visual and auditory hallucinations too, delusions. They say her personality has split and shattered into two. Nothing she thought was real, truly was.

They say Emma is evil, corrupt. A hidden version inside her. Two in one.

They are lying.

Emily is not one part evil, and she can see Emma. She doesn't live inside her own mind at all. She is made of flesh and blood, bone and tricks. She is the dark-haired girl from her childhood all grown up. Emily gave her a name, that was all. Everyone needs a name, or it isn't fair.

The doctors make her swallow pills. Red ones, blue ones, green, pink and yellow. A whole rainbow inside her tummy.

She has to do what she is told. They don't like it when she misbehaves. She is not allowed scissors or sharp things. She is most definitely not allowed crime books.

She lies in her narrow bed in a room of her own. She stares at the wall and wonders how to escape. It must be impossible, on account of all the locks and barred windows. Yet she has to get out, she has to solve the crime and find out who the real killer is.

The police will have to say sorry to her.

Emma sits curled up in the corner. She came in with Emily, into the police car, into a cold cell, and finally, into the secure hospital.

Everyone pretended they couldn't see her.

"What do we do now?" Emily mumbles. "This is all your fault."

Her words are slurred. A side effect from the collection of medicines meant to heal.

"Did you kill them all?" She adds. "Did you do it?"

Emma nods and sniggers loudly. She is proud of herself. She thinks it is funny.

She is a ball of hate, coiled up and ready to strike.

The doctors tell her they will help her make Emma go away forever. She doesn't know what that means, except it might mean that they send her to Australia. It's so very far away. So far that she might not be able to get back.

Right now, Emily hates her, but she doesn't want her to leave. Not now and not ever. It wouldn't be right to send her away or kill her off. She is not a murderer like her.

"I'm very mad at you. But stay with me," she whispers to her. "Don't go. I'm lonely."

The doctors and nurses talk to her in kind tones; they smile at her, but their eyes are narrowed.

Emma crawls over on her hands and knees.

She *is* real. They were born together. They will always be together.

Emma was the one their mother beat as a baby, the one that never woke up from being shouted at and shaken. All that damage hurt Emily inside her mind, but it killed her twin sister.

"Keep me secret and I can stay," Emma tells her. "Trick them, it's easy."

Emily nods and smiles before she falls asleep. Yes, she will do that.

Secrets are better kept inside. She knows this now. She understands and remembers. And why was she ever mad at Emma, anyway? She shrugs; it doesn't matter.

Sometimes, it can be good to forget. Sometimes, it is even necessary.

She is tired, very sleepy.

Life will be good in the hospital, she decides. She has her best friend with her and besides, her mother and all those bad people in her small village are dead.

She smiles.

ONE SUNNY DAY

"A storm's coming," Lydia announces. "I can tell."

I do, of course, roll my eyes. What an odd thing to say, even for her.

It's so hot that it feels as if my clothing has been shrink-wrapped on. I would love it to rain, but it won't and probably won't for months yet.

We've been looking at a castle standing in ruins, my sister Lydia and me. Really, it was just a pile of bricks with a bloody history and one flimsy, lopsided arch.

She booked us a coach trip. A day out, just for the two of us. She insisted I take a break from staring at the walls of my small home, which isn't actually a home anymore. It's become a lonesome house.

Life has been difficult since my divorce. It was vicious and brutal; I suppose all divorces are in their own way.

Still, mine was a cliche too. He ran off, quite literally, with his younger, prettier, and duller receptionist. Off they went, into the sunset, while I was left behind. Broken.

And once things are broken, they're never quite the same. You can always see the cracks and the clumsy line of glue a person uses to fix such breaks. No one ever feels the same about broken things. They're too tarnished.

"I said, there's a storm coming."

Lydia elbows me sharply in the ribs.

"I don't think so," I say.

I look at my phone to check the weather. No signal. That doesn't surprise me. We're in the middle of nowhere. All ruined castles exist in lonely isolation, it seems. Perhaps I too, am a ruined castle with a bloody history.

"It didn't give a storm on the forecast," the burly coach driver, John, tells us.

We all know his name; he made a great point of greeting us and introducing himself. He has huge and sweaty, hairy hands that remind me of great big bear paws.

When we first set off, he promised us we'd all be off on a great adventure. John is a liar and there are only eight of us on the trip, him included.

There's an older couple, a younger couple, and one solitary man with a huge backpack for company. He seemed to enjoy the castle the most.

The coach is equipped for thirty, so at least we have room to stretch out.

"I can tell there'll be thunder. My head feels tingly," Lydia insists. "And look, the birds are acting peculiar."

The birds in the sky are behaving perfectly reasonable to me and besides, statements like that are common for her.

She believes in everything I do not. Aliens, vast conspiracies, Bigfoot, you name it, she believes it. Her cure for any illness is herbal tea and a particular crystal. She sees the world in vivid wonderful colors while I see only black and white shades.

The sky appears clear, wonderfully blue in fact, and it won't be dark for hours yet. There is no storm in sight.

John counts our heads to make sure we all get back on board. Everyone does. Each one of us must be desperate to get home and vow to never book a coach trip again.

I sit in my seat and swallow two paracetamol. My head is pounding. It's the heat. I never have liked summer. I enjoy winter when everything is quiet and miserable. The season matches my personality.

"You haven't eaten," Lydia tells me. "That's why you have a headache. Or your Chakras are out of line. I can tell your aura isn't right, either."

Her seat is behind mine. Even with plenty of room, she feels the need to hover.

"I'll eat when I'm home," I answer. "And my invisible make-believe aura is fine, thank you."

I want to close my eyes and sleep. The coach smells terrible, body odor, and bitter disappointment.

"Shall we get a takeaway together? I could stay at yours, or you can stay at mine. We can have a sleepover. I'll tell you ghost stories! Please say yes, please!"

Hell no. I want to be alone. I want to go back to staring at walls and wondering what might be wrong with me.

"I'll probably just go to bed," I lie.

"Oh."

Lydia falls silent for exactly twenty-nine seconds before she starts up again. Her mouth and brain have to be in constant motion, I swear.

She reaches a hand over my seat and strokes my hair. The feeling reminds me of our mum. She would do the same whenever one of us was upset. My sister knows me all too well. Quiet tears begin to fall.

I want to stop living. I want the world to stop turning. The pain inside grows and amplifies. Time for me only makes the hurt of my broken marriage seem stronger. I feel hollowed out, empty, utterly wretched.

How could his vows and promises mean so little? How could I mean so little?

"Do you think the earth is flat?" Lydia asks.

Oh, for fuck's sake!

"No, Lydia, I do not think the earth is flat."

"I do. I know it's flat. I read this article and I think it's a conspiracy, a government cover-up, and then this scientist on Youtube…"

What follows is an endless speech that makes no coherent sense and defies all natural laws and logic. I nod on occasion and let her ramble. It's a three-hour drive home, and the sun has long since drained me. Stupid castle, stupid coach trip.

I cannot wait to get home and drink wine.

I fall asleep as she talks, lulled by nonsense.

✳✳✳

"Wake up. Something weird happened."

"What?"

"Wake up. Quick."

There's an urgency in my sister's voice. I can hear her apprehension. I open my eyes and see absolute darkness. I cannot remember where I am.

"Hey," she says and shakes me hard.

"Stop it… I'm awake. What happened? What are you doing here?"

"What!"

"What?"

For a moment, my tired mind believes I am in bed and my sister has felt the random urge to break into my house. But no.

We're on a coach. I can recall that much. But why is it so dark? Are we home, or have we broken down?

"Where are we?" I ask. "What happened?"

A breakdown is the obvious answer. Unless we've been delayed somehow. We were supposed to be home by eight, and it should be light outside. How late are we? I was planning on drinking a bottle of white wine all to myself. It's waiting for me in my fridge. It should be cold and crisp and perfect for numbing my feelings.

"We have a flat tire, I think. There was a freaky storm. It was light and then we drove into it, straight into darkness. It was so weird and then the coach just stopped dead! Honestly… weird! I was right though, about the storm. I told you."

I have no real idea what she's talking about. All the same, I rummage for her hand and grasp it tightly.

I feel too disorientated to think properly, but the word weird isn't any cause for alarm. Lydia describes everything as freaky or weird. Even me.

"Where's John?" I ask after a moment.

"I don't know. We pulled up, and he got out with a torch. He said not to worry, but he isn't back yet."

Why hasn't anyone checked on him, or offered to help? Don't any of the passengers watch horror movies?

The driver might be lying dead of a heart attack feet away from the coach and no one knows a thing.

I wipe my face and try to turn my phone's torch app on. Dead. My battery must have failed. It doesn't matter, no one calls me anyway.

"Lend me your phone?" I ask.

"No use. I didn't charge it. 5G melts your brain."

"I… Oh, right."

I have no reply, but I still need a light.

Shit. I know I have a small torch of my own buried inside my bag somewhere. I always keep one handy so I can see to get my key in the lock of my own front door. I often walk in the middle of the night, when everyone is asleep and I'm wide awake.

I rummage until I find the cold metal object, and aim the weak beam around.

Every passenger is still in their seats, all wearing the same anxious but blank expressions, all waiting for someone else to act first. Typical Brits.

"How long have we been parked?" I ask.

"Minutes."

"Why is it pitch black outside?"

"The storm, silly. I told you."

No storm I've ever heard of turns daylight into complete darkness. Was there an eclipse? I haven't paid much attention to the news lately.

Someone needs to find the driver.

"I'm going to look for John," I said. "Stay here."

Lydia is flighty, scared of her own reflection. She jumps at everything and claims a poltergeist lives in her laundry room. Still, she's smart and curious, and younger than me. It's my job to keep her safe.

I begin shuffling my way down the aisle. The whole atmosphere feels strange, electric somehow. The air itself carries a sense of warning. There's an odd smell too, like grass after a downpour of rain.

The blackness outside looks crushing. Have we pulled over inside a tunnel?

The door of the coach is open, and I peek my head out. No tunnel. Only mist and lines of trees facing me. Dark and menacing. Trees always look so sinister at night. Friendly branches lush with leaves in sunlight, morph into twisty limbs reaching out to grab in darkness.

What time is it?

"Has anyone got the time?" I yell.

I hear clothing rustle, people moving to consult their own watches.

"Seven," a male voice tells me. "Oh wait, no. My watch stopped."

"Mine too," says another voice.

What the fuck is happening?

Lydia stares at me. There is a look in her eye I can't place. Fear, yes, but something else, excitement or the spark of an idea.

"Do you know something?" I whisper to her.

"I don't know yet. Maybe a solar flare hit."

"A what?"

"A solar flare. Energy from the sun, similar to an EMP attack. It destroys electronics. Or a nuclear bomb in the atmosphere can cause the same thing."

"Oh," I say. "Right."

I was half expecting her to suggest we'd fallen off the edge of the earth.

Where's that coach driver? He should be in charge and organizing help, not me.

"John?" I shout. "Are you okay?"

Tendrils of cloudy mist are spreading across the ground like searching flickering tongues. It doesn't look right at all. The mist is too thick.

I hear no reply and my voice echoes strangely. Where is he? Were we all so annoying and ungrateful that he ran off and left us?

I aim my light around. We seem to be on yet another country road, a narrow one with a deep ditch at the side. If another car happens to come along, the driver will likely fail to see and hit us.

"Can someone get the hazard lights on?" I shout to the passengers.

People begin to move, eager to help now they've been given a set task. Everyone comes forward and clusters together near the driver's seat.

"Are you going out there?" Lydia asks. "I'm coming too."

"Stay here. He's probably near the engine, fixing something."

I assume the engine is located at the back of the coach and not at the front. I really have no idea. I step down the few stairs and feel a deep coldness engulf me. The sudden change is the equivalent of entering a walk-in freezer. My breath turns to vapor instantly and makes me shiver.

A voice inside warns me that something is very seriously wrong, only I can't figure out what that something might be.

It was bright and sunny, and now this. What the hell happened?

"Does anyone know why we pulled over? Was it a flat tire?" I whisper to the group behind me. It suddenly feels important not to shout.

"No," the older man answers. "The engine failed. It just stopped. I heard it."

"A battery issue?" A woman asks.

"Call the AA," says another.

"No, the RAC is better."

"But the AA is faster."

I stand and listen to the debate, a delaying tactic, no doubt. I don't want to find John or go looking. Everything feels… wrong.

This is the part in horror movies when the first victim dies at the hands of a werewolf or rampaging creature.

"The hazard lights won't come on," Lydia says. "It's all dead. That's not normal."

I know nothing about cars, not one thing. I can't even tell you how to put petrol in one.

I'm thinking hard when I hear a slight sound from the back of the coach. A quick and sharp scuffling noise.

"John?" I whisper.

I wrap my arms around myself and try to sum up the bravery I need.

The only light comes from my pitiful torch. There is no moon, not even any stars have come out to help.

"We might be in a dead zone," I say. "But does anyone have a working phone?"

I don't wait for a reply. I start walking before I can stop myself.

Step by cautious step I go, with nothing but a beam of light for company.

How is this mist so thick? Visibility is almost non-existent.

I put my hand on the side of the coach as a guide. I won't get lost if I can keep hold of the cool metal.

Oh. There's John.

I see two big boots first, toes pointed up towards the night sky as if he decided on a nap. He is not asleep.

He's lying on the road, behind the coach, and he's covered in tangled vines and branches. Except he can't be because that doesn't happen to people, but it has.

Each one has constricted him as tightly as a hungry snake would. There is even one wrapped firmly around his throat. His eyes are bulging and wide open, gazing forever at the starless sky. A look of utter shock is imprinted on his face.

"Oh shit," I say.

How the hell has this happened? Vines aren't capable of springing to life and killing people. They never grow wildly and decide to wrap humans up.

My hands begin to shake, and I feel scorching hot vomit rise. It seems clear we need the police, and fast. I should do something, but I can't move. I'm transfixed by the sight before me. He almost looks cocooned.

Poor old John, with his hairy bear hands, who only ever wanted to show people a castle in ruins.

A sound behind me makes me jolt in terror. Lydia. She grips the back of my t-shirt so tightly it hurts.

"Ouch! That's my skin. Get off!"

"Sorry. Oh! What happened to him!" She gasps.

"I don't know," I say.

My teeth chatter loudly. I want to be sick.

"Fuck."

"Yeah, fuck."

"Shall I check for a pulse?" my sister asks. "How did he get so tangled up?"

I have no answer and it's clear to me that he's dead.

"Don't go near those vines," I warn her. "Get back on the coach."

She ignores me and takes two curious steps forward. I reach out to grab her.

"They're not vines," she whispers. "They're wires."

Perhaps stress has caused my mind to shut down? Maybe I'm lying in an institution and stuck in some kind of medicated dream? Actually, that might be a better scenario than what's happening.

My brain still won't process my sister's words. It's nonsense, except it isn't. I've never believed in impossible things and there is nothing more impossible than thick wires and electrical cables coming to life and attacking innocent coach drivers.

I want to laugh. Our situation feels utterly absurd.

"I still don't understand," the older man tells Lydia. "You didn't see what you think you saw."

"But we did," she argues back and points my torch directly in his face. "Power cords, cables, I don't know. He was covered in thick wiring. Strangled, I think."

"Then he must have slipped fixing something."

I laugh. I laugh wildly and hiccup loudly.

"Sorry," I say when all eyes turn to me. "It's just that…"

I have no idea how to finish my sentence.

We're all back on the coach and I can't even recall climbing the steps or sitting back down, but I guess we did so in a real hurry.

"It doesn't make sense!" A woman wails. "Could this be a prank?"

She has a point, but a colder thought occurs to me, a more rational idea. I've been so shocked that the most obvious thing hasn't occurred to me. Here I am, half believing vines, and then electric wiring came to life when the most brutal answer passed me by.

"Someone must be out there," I say. "Someone killed him and did that to him. It's the wiring from the engine or... something."

"Murderer!" Someone cries in a shrill voice. "There's a murderer!"

This situation would be hilarious if it wasn't so serious.

"Well, I suppose John didn't do that to himself," the old man announces. "It can't be one of us though. We were all in here when he left. Best we lock the door now."

A stampede occurs.

People get stuck in the aisle and wedged in the rush to close the door.

"Calm down!" Backpack man shouts. "Stop!"

There's an authority in his voice and everyone pauses to look at him.

"We're overreacting. What are the chances of the coach breaking down right near a rampaging murderer," he says. "One with wire cutters and cables!"

"No one said he was rampaging," Lydia yells back. She shines the torch his way and gives him his very own spotlight. "He might have gone now, and it could be a trap."

"He?"

"It's always a *he*."

"Is it now?"

"Yes actually. Almost always. Women tend to kill those who've betrayed them, men kill anyone and for lots of different reasons. Some of them even kill for fun, like cats do."

"Yes but... Wait, what?"

"Stop arguing!" I interrupt. "This is madness. We should be trying to get a signal and call for help. Not discussing which gender the killer is or why cats can be assholes."

"You went out there first," the backpack man says. "You might have killed him. Or you might be lying about what you saw!"

What an absurd thing to say. If I was going to kill anyone, it would be my ex and his pesky sidekick.

"Oh piss off," I shout.

"It could be terrorists," the youngest man on board says. "It's always terrorists. They're everywhere, you know. Everywhere. That's what the news says."

He lowers his voice for the last few words as if those particular terrorists are directly outside and listening.

The young woman by his side shushes him. I don't blame her.

We seven are clearly not the kinds of people equipped to deal with strange events like this.

The coach falls silent for a few seconds. The next person to speak is the older woman.

"Listen. There's something out there," she whispers. "I can hear it."

Her words cause an electric shock inside my body. I shiver and stand up because I don't know what else to do. A sense inside me tells me we're all in very serious trouble.

"What did you hear?" I whisper.

In reply, the woman holds up a single finger. Her actions remind me of a teacher trying to silence a class of unruly and noisy children. It works.

I tilt my head to listen. She's right. There is someone out there.

I can hear something heavy shuffling across the tarmac of the country road. Like scratching, only louder.

"Has anyone got a weapon?" Lydia asks. "If *he* gets onboard..."

Backpack man moves away from the group. I figure he must be going to stand in front of us all and protect us, yet he does the opposite. He walks to the back of the coach, sits down, and folds his arms. Twat.

That leaves me at the front. Me. The older man pushes a heavy metal flask into my hands. I catch the soothing scent of coffee.

"Use that," he says, as if things are already decided. Fear has me rooted to the spot.

Lydia, my little sister, my annoying, flat earth believing sister chooses loyalty and stands by my side.

Together, we face the door.

Swish, swish, scrape, scrape, scratch, scratch.

What the hell is it? Who is it?

My mind tries to create rational scenarios. I picture John falling into the engine somehow. What does a coach engine even look like? Does it possess such vicious wiring?

Or did the killer rip it all out and decide to come after us all?

The anticipation, the wait, the sounds, the agony of expectation, makes acid rise in my mouth.

What am I doing? I can't take on a grown man armed with nothing more than a flask of coffee and expect to win. I have no fighting skills; I only have anger for strength.

Swish, scrape, scratch.

Louder. Whatever, whoever it is, is inching closer. No one dares to breathe; we can only listen and wait.

A small thud hits the roof of the coach. We all gasp and look up. I'm holding my breath and it hurts.

We're in deep shit, I know it.

God, I'd kill for a cigarette. Why did I have to quit?

"I'll go and look," The younger man announces. "I'll see who it is."

His sudden words make me jump so hard I drop the flask and whine.

"Idiot!" I gasp.

He pushes past me and races to the door. Yet he only stands and waits. I can still hear the chaotic sound outside. How can such menace and sinister promises be contained within the layers of a noise?

Fuck. I want to be anywhere else but here.

"Back in a minute," the young man announces. "I'm not scared."

He is. I can see the fear in his eyes. It's all bravado from him. All words. He's just as scared as the rest of us.

"What do we do?" My sister whispers to me. A single tear rolls down her face.

"Are we safe?" She adds.

No. Probably not, and I figure we only have two real options.

"We either wait here for help or we run and try to find a car or… a working phone. There must be farmhouses out here?"

"But the wires, the murderer, and it's dark. Oh, and you can't run."

Cheeky cow.

"Wires aren't alive," I say. "And there are no killers out there."

A warm and comfortable lie to soothe myself.

"This is too weird, even for me. I'm terrified."

I almost say me too. I *am* frightened, deeply troubled. I open my mouth to speak and the sudden cry of horror and pain from outside stops me.

"Help! Help me," the voice cries out. "Oh, God!"

No one does a thing. My stomach plummets wildly.

I grip the seat in front and brace for impact. Lydia half jumps on me and everyone bursts into a sudden cacophony of frantic noise.

The young woman the man was with wails like a wounded animal. She jumps up from her seat and runs straight out of the door.

I push my sister off me and do the only thing I can think to do.

I leap up, pull the handle, and close the door behind her.

"You've shut her out!" The others cry. "Open the door!"

I copy the actions of the schoolteacher woman and raise a single finger.

"Shh," I say.

Inherently, I know that neither one of those people is going to be back on board and I want to listen. I need to know what it is we're dealing with.

I hear sounds. Quick frantic swishing noises of something heavy moving swiftly across the road.

Is that sound underneath us?

We all hear quick gasps of terror, terrible screams, and bloody gurgles. Still, no one does a thing.

I see a bright and fierce flash of blue, like miniature lightning, erupt. The sudden color shocks my eyes and makes intricate stains on the backs of my eyelids.

"What the hell is this," I whisper. "What the fuck is going on?"

It looks like an arc of electricity to me, except I'm no expert. I'm not an expert in anything.

Pressure begins to build. My ears pop painfully. Something wicked this way comes. No, don't think that. Maybe a power cable came down? Yes, that's it. That has to be it.

"Lydia... I..."

My words are cut off as we began to tip.

The coach groans loudly. As if the metallic side is going to be torn open like a tin can. I feel the lift, the impossible feeling of the entire coach rising on one side.

People and bags fall in a cascade; we tilt that high. Instinctively, I curl myself into a ball.

No sooner have bodies slammed into the opposite seats than the coach falls back and rights itself with a huge crash and bounce.

Nothing but stillness follows. Did that really just happen?

My mind flatlines.

My body hurts with the sudden impacts. I taste blood in my mouth and realize I've bitten my tongue.

What the fuck is out there? What can do something like that? An escaped zoo animal, some kind of huge predator?

"Is anyone hurt?" Backpack man calls out. His voice wobbles with fright and shock.

I can't see anything, only darker shadows against the all-encompassing blackness.

"Lydia," I cry. She's my only priority. It's urgent that I find her. Where are you, where are you?

I feel her hand clutch mine, her slim, delicate hand with its multiple silver rings. The relief is immediate. She comes crawling towards me on her hands and knees, terror twisting her features.

"Are you hurt?" She sobs.

I don't know; I haven't thought to check. The only question in my mind is how is this even happening?

Someone, the older woman, starts to scream relentlessly. Other voices call out about broken arms and bleeding wounds. The sounds all become one as I struggle to make sense.

Hadn't we all been looking at a castle only hours before? Hadn't we all been disappointed by the sight and eager to get home? The day had been bright and then it wasn't.

Could it be possible I'm still asleep?

I pinch myself hard. It hurts. I'm awake. My heart thuds and skips beats entirely.

Are we going to die?

From outside comes the curious sounds of sharp yet heavy slithering. Sharp quick thuds pound the side of the coach.

This is impossible. I should be in bed with a bottle of white wine and a box of tissues. I should be mourning my dead marriage and feeling sorry for myself. I should be anywhere but here.

Why did I spend so much time wanting to give up and die? I want to live more than anything. My ex was a wanker, anyway. I don't miss him. I have to get us out of here.

"We need to run," I tell my sister. "We need to run now."

"No! There's something out there. A monster, a… I don't know," she says. "But something *really* bad."

No shit.

Now, our options are still two, but a different two. Run like hell or stay where we are and be killed.

Fuck it. No.

I climb to my feet, anger coursing through my body. Blood drips down my head.

I've had enough.

"Listen everyone. There are five of us left. We need to run and go now. Don't think, just do."

"I'm not going anywhere," Backpack man shouts. "We probably got hit by a falling boulder. We're on a country road. It was a rock-slide."

Nonsense, but yet I'm glad he feels the need to stay. Twat.

"Bang on the back windows. Distract it while we run, please?" I ask. "It might buy us time."

"It?" He says.

I don't answer.

The older man and woman are deep in conversation. She's holding a crooked arm to her chest and struggling to breathe.

"We can't go anywhere," the man sighs. "But you go, get help. I'll bang on the windows. Run fast. Get the police."

Lydia shines my torch around.

I can see the faces of the three people we're leaving behind. Fear. Absolute panic and fear. We're dealing with something beyond imagination or dealing with some psychopath with a huge amount of strength. I don't know which answer I prefer.

I've spent so long wanting to give up on life that it became my permanent state of existence. Only by experiencing such a wild event have I understood my desire to live, my yearning to survive. So what I'm divorced, who isn't? I can start again. I'm not going to have my life stolen from me by some freak event.

No, I'm not going to be trapped on some stinking coach by a madman outside.

I won't wait for something incomprehensible to arrive and tear us all to pieces. Fuck that.

I'm going to run, and my sister will be by my side. We're going to survive.

Lydia and I stare at one another. A thousand emotions exchanged within a single glance, in a way that only siblings can do.

"Ready?" I ask. "We run left. Away from John."

She shakes her head, but I see a tiny sliver of determination in her eye. Neither of us wants to be present when the coach is tipped again, or worse, when it rolls entirely.

Selfishly, I want us to live, even if it means sacrificing the others. It's time to believe in myself. I know we can do it.

One, two, three.

I take a deep breath and yank the door handle. It opens inwards with a crunch and jerk.

I can only see blackness. I run forward and hit something solid. I bounce backward and fall in a heap.

What the hell?

"Fuck," I say.

"Yeah, fuck."

The exit is completely blocked.

Wires.

A thick layer of impenetrable wiring covers the entire doorway. There is no way out.

No one speaks.

What can anyone say? Backpack man tries the sunroof, he climbs up on a seat, shoves at it, and punches it repeatedly. No luck. Only a tiny snake-like wire falls inside, a tendril of electrical cord. It has a green glow on the end, and I swear I can feel it watching us.

The emergency exit is blocked too. The windows, a no-go. A closer look with the torch reveals a mass of thick electrical cord is covering the whole coach.

I sit down in my seat and feel the urge to fight. Leave me.

What's the point?

We're in the middle of, or maybe at the end of, an impossible situation. How are any of us supposed to know what to do? And so, we each do nothing.

The older woman cries softly. Her husband wraps his arms around her and remains defiant. Backpack man paces up and down, whispering to himself.

Lydia stares vacantly ahead, for once, quiet. For our entire adult life, I've never asked for her opinion, ever. Any answer was always so far-fetched it hurt my head to even contemplate such wild ideas.

Yet I turn to her. I figure that if anyone has a viable theory or solution, it will be her.

"What is this," I say. "Your best guess?"

She frowns and shakes her head.

"It's not a solar flare. So, another dimension. We drove into another dimension. It's the only thing I can think of. The earth is flat, remember, anything could happen."

Is that even possible? Could there even be proof of other dimensions, with facts and science behind it?

"Are you sure?"

"It was daylight, sunny and then it was dark. In seconds. Only seconds. It was a time storm. Or a portal."

I don't know what that means, but surely such a bad storm has to have an edge, a beginning, or an end? Maybe we just drove into it?

"Help will come, help will come. The military, the police. They'll come," Backpack man mumbles over and over.

A thought occurs to me, an idea from a movie I once saw and thought dull.

"Did we crash?" I ask. "Maybe we crashed and we're all dead. This could be that perjury thing."

The thought chills me the most.

"Purgatory," Lydia corrects me.

"Oh."

But if we really are dead, where is the light at the end of the tunnel Lydia often talked about? Where are our deceased family members, our mother, or our long-ago dead pets? Surely death could never mean electrical wiring and sparks engulfing people and coaches?

No, we are alive. I *feel* alive. There was no crash, only a stop.

I put my head in my hands and try to think harder. Does the floor have an escape hatch? Should we try that?

"What if..." I begin to say.

The floor starts to vibrate, a slow, gut-wrenching build-up of tension.

Earthquake? Rockfall?

No.

The whole coach starts to jerk rapidly.

"Oh shit," Lydia whines. "What's happening?"

A loud buzzing begins. The noise sounds as if a million wasps are outside trying to get in. I feel the vibration inside the marrow of my bones and inside my fillings.

I hold my sister in my arms and wait. I pray to a God I don't believe in to save us all.

The vibrations grow in intensity, the buzzing, furiously loud.

Roaring starts. It's so loud. I feel heat underneath my feet, impossible heat, and then we are rising, rising upwards. My stomach plummets, my insides lurch. Pressure presses me back into my seat.

The shock, the horror, the disbelief, the fright. Knowledge of the impossible.

My heartbeat pounds so fast it feels like one continuous thud of dread. Pressure squeezes my head tighter and tighter. All I can do is hold my limp sister until I blackout.

***

When I open my eyes, I can see beautiful stars. Literal ones, shining in the night sky, glowing in the vastness of space. In desolation.

I can see Earth too, our home, through the tiny gaps between the thick wiring we are surrounded by. It's very far away now.

Blue and white flames burn underneath us. No one knows where we are going, or *why* we are going.

We float. Glide. Weightlessness is beyond horrific.

The older woman never made it. Her husband believes her heart gave out as our coach took off into space. I envy her. Four live bodies and one corpse. He holds her and comforts her as if she is still alive and aware.

Backpack man screams endlessly. He really is such a twat.

Breathing is becoming difficult now.

We are nearing a ship of great size, pulled by forces unknown. The ship is huge beyond imagination, bigger than a city, or even bigger. Sharp-looking, dreadful somehow. Menacing. Tree branches in the dark.

I'm convinced we must be the equivalent of fish, stolen from the oceans by traps and intricate ploys. The wires were our undoing; a net formed around us. A kidnap, a capture, a taking. But for what dreadful purpose? What do we do with the fish we catch?

Lydia is catatonic. She glides with eyes open, but she isn't aware.

I hope I get to tell her the Earth is *not* flat before we die.

Story Notes

The idea for this story occurred on a walk. I take my dog out on very long daily walks and we use country lanes and rugged paths.

I try to use the time for thinking of new plots and characters.

One sunny day, I saw a coach broken down on an isolated patch of road. The burly coach driver was pacing up and down on the phone. Wires were hanging out underneath the coach, or at least, it looked like wiring.

The few passengers were peering out of the windows, expressionless and wide-eyed.

On the way home, the coach was gone, and one single bare electrical wire lay in the place they were.

Now, I'm sure they all made it home safe and sound. But, what if...

AOKIGAHARA

Yokai.

Supernatural entities often imagined as inhabiting a realm between the known and unknown, between chaos and order, light and dark.

Some say they were created as personifications to explain strange phenomena or wild weather, no more than metaphors to describe curious but purely natural happenings.

Others believe that before the time of the Titans, earlier than the Greek Immortals, the Ancient ones existed in flesh, blood, and bone.

Some claim Yokai and Yurei too, were and are real and still exist, perhaps only hidden behind a veil, and given the choice or power to appear at will.

Feeding on fear and deep anguish, they grow in strength and fierce hunger.

Six levels in sacred cosmology, six states of existence, six dimensions, or layers.

Gods, Demi-Gods, Human, Animal, Hungry ones, and Hells.

With a gap or bridge to connect. To seep in through cracks.

Each Yokai was kept in mind, passed down in story by song and warning, in twisted campfire tales, and old folklore.

The many generations before ourselves remembered. While modern-day people forgot their roots and very beginnings. This works greatly in the ancient ones' favor.

One will never defeat a force no one believes exists.

One such Yokai is Jorogumo...

Now

Aokigahara national park is sometimes called the sea of trees. It is a vast forest that sits at the base of Mount Fuji. It is also referred to as suicide forest, and with good reason. The forest is the place many choose as their location to die.

Overwhelmed individuals aim to seek solace in the silence the ground holds, perhaps taking the time to contemplate or truly decide before ending their life. Maybe they each yearn to seek comfort or finality among the trees, boulders, and the long-forgotten paths.

The loss of life in the vast national park became so great that the forest has suicide rangers, made up of employees, and also kind volunteers. It is their job to search and discover the bodies of those who have chosen to leave this existence far behind. Corpses are often found hanging from trees, but it is human bones that are found the most. The forest is home to a good deal of wildlife who enjoy feasting upon the meat of the dead.

Hiroshi is one such suicide ranger. His own brother wandered into the forest years before, weighed down by acute sadness in both his heart and mind. He did not leave the forest; his body has never been found.

Hiroshi mourns him deeply.

Aokigahara is also a popular tourist destination. Many hiking groups visit, lone walkers, people seeking clean and fresh air, and those seeking to meditate alongside nature.

Quite often, people become disoriented and lost. Hiroshi's other job is to locate those lost individuals and guide them out safely.

Currently, there is a British couple missing. They are nine days late for check-in; a long time to be delayed by ordinary issues.

He glances at his paper, and once again recalls meeting the happy pair who were intent on hiking. They were all smiles and excitement. At least, it seemed so.

They grinned and held hands and appeared to be quite in love. Still, it's always so hard to tell who might be at risk the most.

He wonders if perhaps they had a suicide pact; he has seen such things before, many times in fact.

He spreads his map across the old wooden table inside the ranger station and traces the couple's route with a crooked finger. They have already searched for six days in different areas. There is no sign of either person or their belongings.

An older ranger, a weather-worn man, speaks.

"When were they due out again?" He asks. There are often more than one or two people missing, it can be hard to keep track.

"Over a week ago," Hiroshi tells him.

He wonders if one of them might be injured or hurt. A daily search can only be a good thing. Separate grids delegate their search patterns.

The couple logged their intended route and time frame, to prevent becoming lost and forgotten. Yet, they still cannot be found.

"So, we search again today?"

"Yes," Hiroshi tells him.

He feels uncertain. He cannot imagine the nice couple is the kind who came to Aokigahara to die, yet the area has a strange effect on people. He's felt such a thing himself a hundred times.

On occasion, he's sensed eyes he couldn't see watching him. He felt a dark presence, turmoil, and hunger inching closer. Once, he even heard his name being called, yet he convinced himself it was only the wind who chose to speak.

He believes the curious effects might well have been his imagination or an odd result of the many magnetic boulders littering the park. Many scientists have made such claims; that a person can become confused or disoriented in the presence of the huge quartz embedded rocks.

Maybe they're just lost, he thinks. We can find them and lead them out. A happy ending, for once.

"Let's go," Hiroshi says. "We'll find them."

He tries to stay bright and positive. He tells himself the couple definitely wasn't the type to choose suicide.

Still, he knows a person just never can tell.

Before

Carrie watches as a bird flutters lightly and hops across a slim branch. The sight creates a warm glow of love inside her. It's such a simple thing to see, a sight she has seen many times in her life and yet it's so very beautiful. Touching. Nature, she understands, is different, more vibrant once a person takes the time to stop and study.

I adore this place; she thinks.

Her limbs are tired, her muscles ache, and she feels as if a tight band of pressure is wrapped around her skull, but she is happy. Her mind is clear for the first time in several months.

She has no phone signal and no ability at all to check her vital online presence. She half-believed the lack of social media would drive her out of her mind, instead; she feels a new sense of freedom. It isn't as vital as she thinks.

She sits on a crude makeshift log she and James have been using as seating and takes long, deep breaths. It's the mornings she likes best. The day feels full of glorious possibilities.

Peace too. Finding such a rare sensation was the entire point of the trip. Since the couple's arrival in Japan a year before, life has been frantic and loud. Exciting, yes, but far too hectic. There hasn't been time for themselves or for each other.

Visiting Aokigahara has been a dream come true, although James was apprehensive when she first planned the trip. Everyone knew the stories, the myths, and legends, and she can admit she still has a morbid curiosity over the whole suicide forest rumors. But they have seen no dead bodies, found no abandoned camping gear, spotted no lost or aimlessly wandering person. The trip has been and still is, wonderful.

How strange that she should need to find such vast emptiness in order to feel alive and find herself.

"Morning," James says as he climbs awkwardly out of their tent.

Poor James. He loves the trip too, but he is too tall to fit comfortably inside their small tent. Every night, he has to stick his feet out of the tent flap or curl into an awkward ball. A sight Carrie still finds hilarious.

"Morning," she answers. "I made fresh tea."

Water is easy to find. They are camping close to a clear running stream and have a water filter as part of their equipment, just in case.

The camping stove, too, was a great idea. Cooking dehydrated food and making hot drinks is easy.

"Thanks. We need to make our way out today."

As if Carrie has forgotten.

"Yes, I know," she answers and hears the pang of sadness in her voice. She doesn't want to leave. She wants to stay in the friendly forest that has revived her so completely.

"We still have two days and two nights," James reminds her.

He's right. It should take a day and a half in total to backtrack their way to the entrance, and they plan on walking slowly. They have many miles to cover, and it feels good to stop and enjoy the sights.

"Can we come back next year?" She says. "Or later this year?"

James shrugs.

"Work," he mumbles. "Depends."

His words mean no.

He wants to leave Japan and move back home to Britain, but Carrie does not. They are supposed to be working and living in the country for one year only.

It is a point of contention between the two. Usually, their relationship works in harmony, but not on this matter. She understands his homesickness; she suffers from it too on occasion but never the level of loss he seems to feel.

Over the last few days, she *has* been thinking of what life might be like back home and it feels bleak. She adores her teaching job in Japan, loves their home and life, the people and the culture. Her heart wants to stay. She is settled. She expects that he will choose to go home without her. For Carrie, that isn't going to be the end of the world.

Enjoy the last couple of days. I'll tell him I'm staying when we leave.

The scenery around her feels too pretty to spoil or tarnish with the fierce argument such an admission will bring. The land around her deserves love and not the anger and hostility James will throw at her.

Carrie spends a few minutes heating porridge in a saucepan for breakfast before eating and helping to pack their belongings. The environment is so peaceful, sounds other than pretty bird songs are rare. She loves the sensation of hearing nothing and of seeing nothing but lush trees and nature.

She swallows two mild painkillers and stretches her muscles as far as she can. It helps the stiffness a little.

Today will be another good day.

She checks her compass.

They both carry their own, although one of the rangers warned them that compasses might not work around boulders with heavy magnetic qualities.

They must be in a neutral area. Hers is working fine.

James carries a paper map. He insisted on one.

"Are we heading southwest?" She asks.

"I think so. I'll check."

He loves to consult his special map; he's carried it constantly. He lays it on the ground and smooths it out carefully.

That's when Carrie sees her. A slight movement catches her eye.

There is a young girl half hiding behind a thick, gnarled tree. A single delicate hand rests on the rough tree bark and her long hair swings gently.

What! Who is she!

It feels absurd to see a small child in the literal middle of nowhere. The sight is the very last thing she expected to see.

She must be lost.

"James," she hisses. "Someone's there."

"What?"

In the time it takes her to blink, the girl is gone. Vanished.

"I said…" She pauses and holds her hand up for silence. She knows without doubt that she saw the figure.

"Hello?" She yells. "Konnichiwa?"

"You're seeing things," James says. "There's no one out here except us. We're miles away from the set trails."

Carrie doesn't take her eyes away from the tree. The girl disappearing makes no sense. Is she afraid and hiding?

"I said, there's no one there, Carrie."

She feels a swarm of electricity engulf her skin.

There was a girl, I saw her.

She does not believe in ghosts, in sinister hauntings, or hungry ghosts eager for life once more. She only believes in what she can see, and she knows there *is* a girl and she must be shy or fearful. Perhaps something terrible has happened to her, and that's why she is hiding. It's the only explanation she has.

She steps forward.

"Hello," she calls again. There is no reply, not even from the gentle wind around her.

Yet someone is watching. She can feel the curious knowledge hit her senses.

James stands up, towering over her as always, and squints in the direction she stares.

"There's no one out here," he repeats. "Your eyes are playing tricks."

What an absurd saying, as if her eyes can work independently and decide to play pranks on her brain for their own amusement.

Carrie wipes her face. Perhaps he's right. A trick of the light? Tiredness? Or maybe her mind conjured the girl. Perhaps ghosts exist after all? If anywhere should be haunted, it is Aokigahara forest.

James is a believer in all things paranormal. He should have been the one to witness the child, not her.

She walks towards the tree and peers around it. He is right, there is no one.

***

In bright daylight and walking with the sun on her back, it is easy to believe her imagination ran away with her. She must be more exhausted than she thinks. She pushes the encounter far away into the back of her mind. Even so, the image she saw keeps creeping back into her thoughts.

Step by careful step they walk. James is striding ahead, humming quietly, lost in his own thoughts and she follows closely, as lost inside her mind as him.

The ground feels quite flat. Although it is gently sloped, it's important to watch out for rocks that might trip her. Still, it's hard to concentrate.

Everything looks the same.

From the beginning of their hike, they chose to leave the set trails and discover their own route. It is not something a person is supposed to do. There are multiple warning signs forbidding such off-trail exploration. But they are both experienced hikers seeking peace and adventure. They saw nothing wrong with their plan.

An undisturbed and wild forest, they believed, should be seen.

"Carrie, stop," James says.

"Why?"

Her reflexes react slowly. She almost collides with his backpack. What has he seen? Is there a lost child after all?

"There's an old camp, look."

"Oh no."

She feels a jolt of alarm. She is curious by nature, yes, but she doesn't want to see a dead body hanging from a tree like the rumors often speak of. Especially one that might be skeletal or rotten.

"I don't want to look!" She says and closes her eyes.

There might be a vision she will never be able to unsee. A terrible sight might stain her eyelids and every time she closes her eyes, it will be there, waiting for her.

"It's okay, it's an abandoned camp. Come on, we'll mark the location and tell the ranger. It might belong to one of those missing people, like in those posters we saw."

The ranger station had hundreds of flyers scattered across the walls like unusual wallpaper, all containing the faces of the many lost and vanished inside the forest borders.

She opens one eye and follows the direction of James's pointed finger.

It truly is an old campsite. The red tent looks stained and weather-worn. One side is ripped and torn in ribbons. Damage caused by wildlife, no doubt. The ruined shreds catch in the wind and flicker gently.

The two step closer.

An old fire pit sits close to the tent; the flames long since died. One single rusty tin can and a saucepan sit aside it.

James drops to his knees and peers inside the tent. Carrie holds her breath.

"Empty," he announces.

Thank God!

She looks around as if expecting the owner to be present. In reality, the person must be long ago dead if that was their intention, or they could have changed their mind and left. Maybe they were just camping and abandoned their things for some other reason?

She notices a tree with Japanese symbols carved neatly into the bark.

But what does it mean? Her knowledge of the Japanese language is barely passable. She teaches English to English-speaking students. She can speak the language, yes, but only enough to get by, nothing more.

Is it someone's name? Or a message?

"James," she says. "What does that say?"

He is more fluent than her. Surely, he understands? He follows her gaze, frowns, and shrugs.

"I don't know. Sorry."

I should take a photograph for the ranger.

It could be someone's very last words or thoughts. Or at least, a name.

She feels certain her camera still has some power left. If not, she has batteries spare. She only needs to find them.

She drops her pack and feels immediate relief from the weight. She rolls her shoulders and takes a deep breath.

"Friends?" Asks a soft voice from behind her.

Carrie shrieks in alarm. Immediately, she jumps and spins around.

There was a girl! I knew it.

But the woman before her is no young child. She is very small and slender, but older than Carrie first believed. She is wearing a dirty white dress and has bare feet. Nothing about her looks appropriate for wandering the forest. She almost looks as if she stepped straight from the pages of an old fairy tale book.

Her long black hair has several small branches caught and tangled up in knots. Her face is filthy. Mud or grime of some kind covers her cheeks.

She looks utterly distressed and thoroughly sorry for herself. She shivers deeply.

"Oh my God," Carrie says. "Are you okay?"

She takes off her plaid shirt and steps forward.

"Here, wrap this around yourself," she says. "Are you lost? What happened to you?"

She automatically assumes the woman must have wandered away from a group and become confused.

Poor thing, she must be terrified! We're miles from the entrance. How long has she been out here?

"Friends?" The woman asks again. She reaches for the shirt but lets her thin arm fall back down.

"Yes, of course. I'm Carrie, and this is James," she points to her confused boyfriend.

"We're all friends and we'll help you find your group or a way out."

They can't be far away.

"Carrie," James says. "What the fuck are you doing?"

"I'm helping her; what does it look like?" She snaps back.

Gosh, he can be so heartless sometimes!

"Helping who?"

"The woman!"

"What woman?" He says.

Perhaps he can't see her from the angle he's crouching down at? Carrie looks back to beckon the woman forward. But she is gone, as if she was never there, to begin with.

Her legs give out and she sinks to the ground.

She feels as if a bucket of freezing cold water has been tipped all over her. She is shaking rapidly. Confusion, fear, shock, disbelief all fight for first place inside her mind.

The place she loves, the place she didn't want to leave, now feels hostile. An enemy or traitor forest.

I saw her. I know I did.

The woman was flesh and blood. She had detail and vibrancy. She spoke. Her bare feet touched the ground.

"Honestly, nothing blocked my view. There was no one there," James says. "I'm sure there's a rational explanation."

"She was real!" Carrie sobs as she struggles to breathe. "She was right there, I swear!"

This makes no sense.

"Are you hallucinating?" He asks. "You didn't touch those weird-looking mushrooms, did you?"

He raises a hand and presses it to her forehead as if a fever might be the best way to tell if she had.

"No! Because I'm not an idiot!" She says and pushes his hand away.

"Okay, okay. It was just a thought."

James rubs his face over his stubble and sighs loudly.

"I want to leave," Carrie says.

For her, it suddenly feels vital that they should get out of the forest and do so quickly.

The alarm bells of her instinct are shrilling loudly.

"We *are* leaving."

"No, I mean, I don't want to spend another night here. We need to leave today. Now. I spoke to a woman, right there," she points. "And you say you couldn't fucking see her. It's just not possible. Fuck!"

James rummages in his pack for his precious map. Carrie can only sit on the hard ground; her legs feel boneless and weak.

What about the water? Was there something in the water? Am I sick?

While his back is turned, she checks her own forehead for a fever. No. She has a normal temperature.

She knows what she saw, but she cannot explain why James failed to see her. The threads in her mind won't connect.

What if he did see her and he's lying? But why? Stop it! That makes no sense.

All the same, the gut-wrenching feeling of paranoia begins to rise.

The woman was real. She could practically feel her body heat.

"Look, we're miles away from the entrance. It's a day and a half of hiking, at least," James tells her. He points a finger across the map and follows the route they marked out.

"Then we'll hike through the night. It'll be faster," Carrie answers.

"Absolutely not. One of us *will* have an accident."

The way he says the words makes her skin hiss. He almost sounds as if an accident will be a certainty. Or a promise.

Stop it, I'm being foolish. I must have imagined her. But why?

When they make it out, she decides she will go to a doctor and find out why she conjured up such a woman. She will ask for a test of some kind, to see if the water contains odd things it shouldn't.

But the explanation doesn't feel right. She has heard stories of strange visions, ghost sightings, and supernatural women only appearing to other women, often as a warning. Could that be what she saw? Is she in danger?

I don't believe in ghosts.

Yet not believing doesn't make the dead appearing any less a powerful event.

Okay. What if she was a ghost? What else could she be?

Carrie knows she was a vivid woman, not a shadow or a shade, not see-through or floating.

"She was a ghost," James says, as if reading her mind. "That's what she must have been."

Carrie shakes her head and then nods. It feels absurd to agree with him. Ghosts are for old graveyards and derelict haunted houses, asylums, and the sites of terrible wars. The dead aren't for pretty forests in the bright daylight. Are they?

The shock of acknowledging such a thing makes her head spin. Should they fear the dead that inhabit the forest? Is it a new life they seek? Was she a hungry one?

"If it was a ghost, are we in danger, am I?" She asks. "You know all about this stuff, not me."

"No. There's more to fear from the living than the dead. That's what my mum used to say, and she was right, I think. Listen, what if she was a recording playing out?"

"What?"

To her, it sounds as though his words are madness contained within a sentence.

"There's a theory, it's called Stone tape theory. People say events get recorded somehow onto the environment. With all these boulders around, it wouldn't be surprising. It might not have been a ghost, but an old scene playing out again."

Carrie understands a little, but it all sounds too creepy to her and far too unlikely.

The woman looked her in the eye, and that was no replay. They connected in the here and now. And the shirt, she almost took her shirt.

Images of Japanese horror movies begin to play inside her mind, black-haired women crawling out of abandoned wells and across ceilings, seeking revenge.

She shivers violently. Fear swarms inside.

Why isn't he worried or afraid?

"James, how can you act so casually?"

"I didn't see anything. Sorry Carrie, but I think it only happened inside your head."

The breath leaves her body. How could he think and say such a thing?

He doesn't believe me.

"What if she came to warn us about something?" She asks.

"What could she warn us about? We're safe out here."

Are we?

It doesn't feel as if they are.

"I want to go," she whines. "Let's get as close to the entrance as we can. There might be people around. Hikers or campers."

"Come on, then."

James pulls her to her feet. He checks his compass as she breathes slow deep breaths and tries to control her shaking limbs.

Everything is fine, everything is fine, her mind chants.

"Which way?" He asks. "My compass is spinning."

The boulders! Of course! Did they have an effect on me, too?

She decides it's something she wants to research as soon as they get home. She will search for answers then. But the realization makes her feel comfortable. If the boulders somehow made her hallucinate, then there are no dead wandering. There is no dire warning.

She reaches into her pocket and finds her own compass.

Hers is spinning wildly too.

"When I saw the abandoned camp, it was on my left, so we should keep going forward."

"Are you sure?" Carrie asks.

"Yeah," James says, without a shred of doubt in his voice.

For the first time, she wishes they had hiked along the set paths and trails like people are supposed to. An adventure seemed like a great idea at the beginning. Many people visit the forest, especially in summer. Neither one of them wanted to be bumping into hikers every few miles. No, they wanted peace and isolation, but now look, they're lost.

The woods and trees around her appear menacing and everything looks the exact same. Tree after tree after tree. The beauty she found so wonderful is absent and fled away entirely. Perhaps it was all a lure to entice. A trick of nature.

She already feels exhausted, from shock and fear, no doubt. Anxiety and terror nibble away at her insides.

Her limbs are like lead, her backpack heavier than she recalls. She cannot shake the feeling of impending doom.

James sets off ahead, and she dutifully follows, walking two steps behind. It is tough for her to keep pace, and her stomach rumbles with hunger.

We're not stopping for food. Not a chance.

They wind around thick spiky bushes, and boulders sitting around like the forgotten marbles of a giant.

Through a cluster of thick trees and down a wide, long slope lined with bushes and berries.

James stops abruptly.

"My compass still isn't working. I think we're going the wrong way."

"What! You said it was this way."

"I know, I'm sorry. I think we should double back. Come on, it won't take long."

Not long? It will mean a wasted hour of sunlight, at least.

Panic grips her tightly. Everything feels wrong. How can their trip have changed so much? She was happy and free when she woke, unchained and serene. Now she feels frantic, condemned somehow.

The forest that lured them with its wildness and provided comfort for days is now against them.

She peers around. Nothing at all looks familiar, but then why would it, whoever notices the positions of boulders and rocks and remembers the details? It feels as if the trees are moving. She is sure they are closing in and seeking to crush her.

Calm down, breathe, breathe.

She closes her eyes. She wants to scream. This is all James's fault. He swore he knew the way.

"You have that paper map," she says. "You said this was easy."

"Then you do it!"

"Fine, I will," she snaps. It seems as if her own boyfriend has joined the trees and turned against her, too.

She drops her pack once more and feels utterly surreal.

How can we be so lost?

The sun will go down soon, and darkness will arrive. The blackness might hold all manner of terrible things. She will lie awake in their tent and listen for sounds coming closer. She will listen for the woman, but what if she hears her, then what?

"Carrie, look at this."

She jumps at the sound of his voice.

James is pointing to a solitary vicious-looking bush rich with thorns. Red berries decorate the green and make it look Christmasy and jolly. It is absurdly out of place.

The top of the bush is covered in a thick spider's web. She stumbles forward for a clearer look. She isn't afraid of spiders, but what kind of spider could make such a thing? It's so thick it almost resembles a blanket.

James glances up, and she follows. Over their heads, a canopy of white spreads out like a ragged boat's sail. The individual strands each look like white wool or cotton.

"What the hell?" Carrie says. Her fear levels climb several notches.

She becomes deeply afraid.

What appear to be small animals are cocooned and heavily wrapped inside the web. Perhaps rabbits or hares? But that, she knows, is impossible.

"We need to go," James whispers.

The fear-drenched look on his face tells her all she needs to know.

She doesn't argue. She snatches her pack from the ground and yanks his hand.

"Quick," he breathes. "We need to go quickly."

The two run until she feels her lungs burn in protest. She tries to lead them both in a straight line and yet it feels like they're racing around in circles.

She has never felt such clarity of fear, even the wild turbulence and the screams of passengers on the plane flight over was less frightening.

"Stop!" James calls. "We're going to get even more lost."

How can they stop? First came a ghost woman only she could see and next, massive and unnatural spider webs. They need to speed up, not stop.

James does not agree. In the middle of a small clearing, surrounded by ancient trees, he drops his pack and sits down. His breathing is harsh and uneven.

Shit.

"James, please. We have to keep going," she begs.

He only holds up a hand in reply. She has to wait and hops about from foot to foot.

Shall I leave him behind? Can I?

No. She won't. She would never forgive herself if he disappeared.

"I got spooked," he finally says. "I'm sorry. Listen, it's all just a coincidence. Do you know anything about spiders in this country, really? Because I don't. What we saw might be normal."

He must be kidding!

How can anything that's happening be considered normal? She is the rational one; he is the one who believes in wild things that make no logical sense. How have their roles reversed polarity so easily?

Something is seriously wrong. The rumors of the forest are truth and fact, not urban legends after all. It is a damned place.

They should never have stepped inside the ruthless grounds. The whole area waited for them to relax and drop their guards before it pounced.

The forest is haunted by hungry ones, or at the very least, something evil.

"I'm serious Carrie, we're running for no reason."

She walks over and crouches down beside him. He looks bitterly tired, fearful, and utterly defeated.

"Then run for me. We have to get out of here. Can't you feel something bad is here? I'm so afraid."

The moment she speaks the words, she understands it is the truth, regardless of her rational beliefs

He clutches her hand and looks up, but his eyes don't focus on her. Instead, they widen sharply, and he gasps.

"I can see her," he says.

She immediately spins.

The woman is standing feet away, smiling shyly.

"Friends?" She says. "My friends?"

***

Carrie watches the stranger with narrowed eyes. Clearly, she has followed them.

At first, she longed to help her and now she yearns to keep her as far away from them as she can get.

The woman is sitting cross-legged on a boulder beside them. James has set up the camping stove and is boiling water for tea. They exchange looks frequently, both trying to convey messages without voices.

"Friends?" The woman repeats.

The word is beginning to annoy Carrie. Deep inside her, her instinct is warning her of terrible things ahead.

No. She's lost. That's all. Like us.

Yet how can she explain why James couldn't see her before? Maybe she truly was shielded from sight by the trees. It's the only explanation she can think of and yet it doesn't feel correct. She is forcing herself to believe a lie.

We can't abandon her, it's too cruel. She might die.

Yet that's exactly what Carrie wants to do, leave her behind and run.

"Do you speak English?" James asks her.

"Friends?"

"That's a no then. Can you help us get out of the forest?"

He points wildly, as if she might understand.

The woman tilts her head in concentration and frowns. She looks so sweet and gentle, harmless in fact. She raises her arm, points a slender finger into the deeper woods, and smiles.

"Friends."

This time, her word is not a question, but more of a statement.

"I think she means her friends are that way?" James says. Carrie nods her head; it does sound that way but is it really a good idea to go wandering deeper into the woods with the strangest of all strangers?

"They could help us find our way out," James adds.

He passes Carrie a drink of tea and pushes one into the hands of the woman. She peers at it curiously before dipping a finger into the hot liquid.

"Oh!" She gasps.

Carrie shuffles backward and widens her eyes at James.

She's acting as if she doesn't know what a cup is, or hot tea!

James looks just as confused as her, but shrugs.

"A culture thing, I guess?" He says.

"Are you seriously suggesting Japanese people don't know what a cup is!"

"Shhh, Carrie."

"Why? She can't understand me. James, we should go and just leave her here. We'll tell the rangers; they can come back and get her."

"You're overreacting. We'll find her friends and they'll help us leave."

No fucking way.

"You've seen too many horror movies," James laughs.

Patronizing idiot.

She folds her arms, and watches as the woman tips her drink upside down and giggles.

She's insane, that's what she is. I'm not going anywhere with her.

Ten minutes later, she finds herself trailing after James once more.

He is keeping pace with the woman who is behaving as if the forest is her permanent home or part of her. She seems to know every decent path and barely visible trail. She skips along with ease.

Turmoil is spiraling around inside herself. The situation feels absurd. She wonders if they are walking straight into a trap of some kind.

No, we'll find a camp with good people. Everything is fine. They'll help us.

Daylight is beginning to fade; the shifting colors are darkening slowly, and the temperature is dropping. The forest feels as if it is preparing to come alive.

Her stomach growls with hunger.

How much further?

"Friends!" She hears the woman clap delightedly.

James stops and drops to his knees. Carrie assumes he has tripped and reaches for him; she almost laughs at his clumsiness. He retches loudly and pushes her back.

"What? What's happening?"

She peers over him and sees a body lying face-up on the cold ground.

A thousand thoughts cross her mind and then none at all. She cannot understand what it is she's seeing.

The woman points to the body and giggles softly.

"Friend," she says.

The body is weeks old or perhaps more. The skin of the corpse is mummified and gray. Tight and wrinkled.

It's been ripped wide open, and the ground is stained dark red. The insides are missing entirely. A line of intestines trails out and looks for all the world like a link of dried sausages. Thousands of tiny, white and slimy eggs like frogspawn are nestled underneath the picked clean rib cage.

"What the fuck!" Is all she can think to say. Her mind fills with white noise. The sudden severity of the sight is too great.

She grabs at James and stumbles blindly.

"Up," she tells him. She only knows that they need to get far away as fast as they can.

The woman giggles and places a delicate hand over her mouth. She has caused enough fear and grown stronger for it. She jerks and abruptly drops onto all fours. The sound of clothing ripping and muscle popping fills the forest.

Carrie falls down, mind and body. She becomes a witness to the impossible.

The woman roars in anguish, but there is power and strength inside her wails of pain. She throws her head back in triumph, gripped by some kind of wild, frantic seizure.

Bulges explode from her flesh, from her sides and abdomen. The bulges elongate furiously quickly into long, coarse hair-covered legs.

Carrie cannot move, she is frozen in absolute shock. She can only stare with eyes wide. Beside her, James whimpers and begins to crawl away.

The woman shrieks, a brutal, wretched sound, and rears backward. Her hands grab and clutch the air. Several fully-formed long legs hit the ground with heavy thuds. Long fangs explode savagely from her mouth. Bones popping, gristle snapping, nerves shredding, tearing, rearranging, transforming.

From her head to her lower chest, she is still a woman. From waist to feet, she is a creature, some kind of twisted eight-legged being. A spider woman. The car-sized monstrosity writhes and hisses. She is ancient and utterly terrifying, made up of pure muscle and perhaps dark spells or the blackest of magic.

She rears back on six of her legs and jumps, leaving a blanket of perfect white spread out behind her. Carrie is her target, and she stands no chance at all. She has no time to think, no time to scream, no time to act. No time to regret.

Within seconds, she is cocooned from head to foot in strong, thick webbing.

James scrambles up and runs. He leaves her behind.

He races over fallen branches, saliva falling down his chin. He runs at a furious sprint, desperately searching for anything familiar, any track or path. He sobs in horror. He left her; he left Carrie, the woman he promised to love and protect.

Yet what could he do?

He has no intention of going back.

He can't breathe, his lungs hurt. Dizziness engulfs him until flashing black spots burst across his vision.

He stops and leans against a tree. He won't let his life be over, he won't allow it. Not like this.

The ground under his feet starts to vibrate. She is coming, that thing is coming for him. He searched behind him, nothing.

"HELP," he shouts. There is no one to help him. No human ears to hear.

He is praying there might be someone close enough to become alerted to his shouts.

Two deep breaths and he sprints again. Pure survival instinct propels him.

His heart feels like quick gunfire bursts.

Wait, that rock face. Didn't they walk past it on their way in? It seems like a lifetime ago, but he feels sure he knows the sight. It's jagged and shaped like a face. Yes! It is the one. He knows it; he remembers.

He must be close.

He jumps over an old log and ducks under a low branch. Bushes and thorns tear at his skin. He barely notices.

I'll find people, I'll get help, I swear, his mind chants. We'll go back, I'll save her.

No.

James lies to himself. He will never set foot in the forest again; he only intends to send others.

He sees a bright flash of white and collides with a hanging branch, hitting his head with the impact.

A sheet? His scrambled mind assumes.

Blood drips down his face. It takes him only seconds to realize he cannot move. His body is bound tightly.

He screams into the empty forest. No one hears.

But where is that wretched sight? That thing.

A rustling sound comes from above him. He cranes his head as far as he can. He needs to see. The huge spider woman is making her way towards him.

Creep, creep, creep. All stealth, slow motions, gentle poise, and dread. Long legs move with ugly grace and purpose.

She still has the upper body of the woman, and she smiles so very sweetly.

"Friend," she says.

I'm trapped in a web. I'm in her web.

The impossible knowledge bends his mind too far and his sanity snaps. He screams and wails as the spider woman drops down gently and wraps him in her dark embrace. She has eggs that need a warm place to hatch. She needs a friend.

Now

Hiroshi hears the whistle of his companion and fellow searcher. He stands and follows the sound.

A backpack. A single backpack lays at the other ranger's feet. It is red and blue and looks familiar.

"Is it theirs?" He immediately asks. "Is it?"

He feels his stomach flip with anxiety while he waits. He is tired of mourning strangers and sometimes it hurts as much as if they were his own family.

The two rangers have been searching for the nice couple for several days. Although they have found three abandoned camps and clothing belonging to others, they have found no trace of the British pair. Until now.

The ranger sighs and nods his head.

"Yes, and look, there are a few bones."

The hope Hiroshi feels dies a quick death. He feels tears well up in his eyes and shakes his head to free them. It's all just too sad. No doubt the national park's many natural predators had a feast on the dead and scattered the remains.

He steps forward. Yes, there are many bones, small and big. They will collect everything they find, but it's likely the university that will examine the bones will be unable to find a cause of death. How can they? With no actual body left behind.

He guesses the pair must have had a suicide pact after all. Still, at least they can use clever DNA techniques to identify them.

"Is there a note?" He asks.

"Maybe in the backpack," the ranger says.

He bows with respect and lets the sadness settle inside him. He wishes he could spot the ones who are intent on dying in the forest and yet it's just too hard to tell. Those who wear such wide smiles are often the most broken inside, it seems. The forest swallows them so greedily.

On a tree he glances at, he sees a symbol carved into the bark.

Yokai territory.

That's what it means.

He sighs, he wishes people wouldn't hurt the trees or graffiti such silly things. Especially words of such superstitious old non-sense...

THE DISCARDED ONES

Now

'Ring-a-ring-a-rosies, a pocket full of posies, a tissue, a tissue, we all fall down.'

While her skull pounds with waves of agony, her brain sings her mother's favorite song, a soothing melody, a nursery rhyme from a time long ago, in the days when pretty roses still existed. She does not know why her mind chooses this particular song. It is hardly appropriate. There are no roses, posies, and certainly no tissues to be seen. Although she has indeed fallen down.

The woman with the nursery rhyme playing in her mind, Lucy, understands that her thoughts are tangled, muddled up and back to front.

Why is she thinking so hard about pretty flowers? She clearly has a serious problem. She is injured, but what happened?

Knowledge of recent events hits her all at once. Memories play and collide with brutal force.

She tries to sit up, but the pain in her head only increases. Panic rises.

She wonders if she has been punched or shot? Yes, a bullet, that might be the answer. Maybe a smooth yet lethal piece of metal has pierced the layers of her brain until she finds herself malfunctioning like a renegade artificial intelligence. If a bullet isn't jammed inside her skull now, one soon will be.

"Fuck," she says.

Blood drips down her face and briefly blocks her vision.

She blinks rapidly until her eyes decide to cooperate and focus.

Has he gone?

No. Of course not. Why would he leave? He isn't done.

The man in black stands over her. He raises a booted foot and places it firmly on her chest as if he is afraid she might vanish or fall through a tiny crack in the metallic floor and escape him.

It is at this very moment that Lucy understands she is about to die.

She waits for her life to inevitably flash before her eyes, yet nothing comes.

How typical, that she, of all people, has to miss out on viewing her short life one last time. Maybe there was nothing of value to see. Still, there is now. *Now* she has value. She will be legendary. The tables are turning, spinning, in fact.

She laughs.

"What's so funny," the man in black asks.

He half growls his words in that rough way of his. There is pride in his voice, power. He has beaten her, and she knows this all too well, yet has he?

There is a larger game at play than the cat and mouse between them.

He is head to toe in black, with most of his face covered, and she still knows who he is by his cruel eyes. Ironic that he should be the one to end it.

"Pull the damn trigger," she hisses like a snake. A dangerous, cornered snake. She cares no more.

"End it."

She wants it all to be over. Pain, life, experience, consciousness, all of it. She wants to fade into oblivion and cease to be. Perhaps the universe will recycle her, and she will be born again into a kinder world. Or maybe not.

It was all such a hopeless plan to begin with.

What fools they all were, thinking a new start would be any different. Sins can never be left behind. They are carried within; she knows this. Sins and deceit are embedded into the very cells of human beings, corruption too. There is no escape from what they are. Their leaders are warlords dressed in fancy suits of silk and fine cotton instead of metal armor.

Did they all hear me below? Did they understand?

As if in reply and perhaps it is, an alarm begins to sound. A quick loud pulse signaling imminent danger and chaos.

It is too late for some. The mighty will come tumbling off their golden perches.

'A tissue, a tissue, we all fall down.'

Lucy begins to laugh harder.

Her voice is drowned out by the siren. It sounds like a call to arms, a war cry. For her, the sound is justice rising. A tsunami of revenge, of wrath.

"You fucking idiot," the man gasps. "What did you do?"

He knew she was trouble; he sensed such a thing, and he was right.

He is shaken. She can sense the worry in the tones of his voice. Perhaps he too will meet his end soon.

Lucy tastes blood in her mouth, the agony she feels is spreading like spilled oil. Her body becomes colder, she shivers.

Truly, she hoped to see beauty once last before she died. But she won't.

All she sees is the end of a brutal weapon, a gun pointed at her head, an ugly sight, the worst vision of all. She is glad that at least she saw great wonders once.

She is not afraid.

She closes her eyes and tries hard to picture a flower. A single solitary rose with multiple spiky thorns. How pretty they must have looked.

"I said, what did you do?" This time, there is fear and savagery in the man's voice.

"Freedom," she laughs and spits up a torrent of blood. "A bomb. Boom!"

'Ashes in the water, ashes in the sea, we all jump up with a one, two, three.'

So it is an appropriate song after all, but it will not be her doing the jumping. She will be the ashes in a sea of infinity.

The man glances at the body lying beside her and sneers. All that blood and only half of it belongs to the rebellious woman with trouble for bones.

She has to be executed. She failed to obey. There are rules. She killed a man too.

"Murderer," he says and pulls the trigger.

Before

The wake-up alarm shrills loudly.

It is impossible that four hours have passed so quickly. For Lucy, it feels as if she just closed her eyes and now, she has to force them open once more. It is a furious battle she has to win.

Her body needs rest, and she hurts. Her limbs throb in protest. Even her toes burn in pain.

She is sick.

Sick and tired. No, not just tired, bitterly exhausted.

The groans of her workmates surround her. They each feel as she does, and each one is just as trapped as her.

"Another day, another dollar," someone says.

But that's a lie. There are no dollars, not for them. Payment is the gift of survival, the knowledge of hope.

She swings her legs out of her hammock and, being careful not to fall onto the people below her, climbs down the short ladder and drops onto the hard floor.

The impact hurts her knees. She feels ruined. Anguish spreads.

She is only twenty-two years old.

"Eight minutes," a loud machine-like female voice announces over the system.

There are twenty-five bodies in the small but tall room. They hang in hammocks like cocoons. The room is one of hundreds. The worker's quarters. The vital workforce.

The rooms were advertised as spacious. Another lie. By the time they were all on board, it was too late to see the truth and too late to leave. The only exit is out into the frozen space surrounding them, space they never get to see.

Lucy dresses quickly. They all sleep in their temperature-regulated suits but all the same, she wraps a thin jacket around her shoulders and slides her blistered feet into tough boots. The pain makes her gasp. It is both exquisite and blinding.

"Seven minutes."

A wave of rage builds. She wants so much to find the woman who speaks or find the computer that counts down without a shred of compassion. She wants to smash it until nothing but tangled wiring remains.

"Come on, hurry," a man says behind her.

She yearns to say she won't. She longs to say she can't. She wants to go back to sleep and dream about what Earth used to look like before it died.

She has seen pictures, recordings of the world from before. When people lived on the surface and took such a privilege for granted.

To her, it all looked so glorious and beautiful. She could imagine a warm sun and sandy beaches. She could dream of gorgeously tanned people in California, a place she wishes she could have seen for real or a national park. How beautiful it all must have been.

Instead, she nods once and hurries.

Obedience is valued.

"Six minutes."

Obey.

Her mouth feels like the sand she dreams of.

There is no time for a drink. They all have to make do with the vitamin tablets the machines give out. Each one contains all the hydration and nutrition a person needs.

At least, that's what they're told.

Lucy thinks they might be poison. She half believes those in charge are killing the brain cells of the workers until nothing but compliant robots remain. Human shells, devoid of thought. Slavery in deep space.

The door unlocks and slides open.

She joins a stream of thousands, all heading towards a twenty-hour day of hard work. Not just hard work, back-breaking, soul-crushing work. Each moment is sheer misery. Agony.

Still, the only alternative is death.

For her, dying feels like it might be a pleasure. At least then, her body can rest.

Yet she is one of the chosen few. One of the lucky.

***

Millions applied, and only thousands were accepted.

Back on Earth, gaining a position on the huge ship The Destiny brought her glory she didn't want. Her handful of friends were wracked with jealousy. The family members she had left alive were proud.

It was her escape. A way for her to live. Freedom beckoned. The chance to begin again with a purity of heart, alive under clear skies and surrounded by vivid and new nature.

A one-way trip to colonize a beautiful Earth-like planet, unimaginatively titled Terra-Two.

The job offer was a dream come true, although she lied. Lied until she passed the aptitude test, the health check, the psychological profiling.

Yes, she would be compliant. Yes, she would always do as she was told.

Obey, obey. No complaining, no questions.

Yes, she would work for the four years it took to travel. Yes, she understood it would be hard and finally yes; she understood failure meant a lone trip of her own out of the airlock.

There was no room on board for anything other than resilience.

Earth would die. As they left, its surface was already unable to sustain life. Those underground would perish soon enough. The last generation. Poisoned air for tired lungs.

The great ship The Destiny represented survival; hope, and she had a place on it. Enough room for exactly 14,000 people in total.

A futuristic rapture made possible by great scientific minds and machines. A mass exodus.

Humanity would live and maybe even thrive.

Promises were made. Rules were set on how to create a new society of equality.

Everyone would be the same in the new world. No elite. No corruption.

There would be no wealthy, and no poor. No one with less and not one soul with more.

People were set to be in charge, yes, but chosen leaders. Singled out by a fair voting system and with crucial decisions made by all.

Humanity could be whoever they wanted to be without suffering scorn or judgment.

They would have friendship and exploration inside their hearts. Peace and kindness.

It would be paradise.

Redemption.

***

Three years and two days left; Lucy thinks. *Three years and I'll have the rest of my life to enjoy. I can do this. I'm lucky.*

She is lying to herself.

Already, she feels her mind untethering. There is no escape. Salvation is as far away as the planet they travel to, and each day is exactly the same as the one before it.

The mountainous ship runs on Ion drives. The end of the world came too fast for grander, more intricate designs or faster than light capabilities.

Internally, conditions are brutally hostile. A curious dark substance others nicknamed Coal-two is constantly shuttled into a large furnace. They are told the substance is essential. Lucy has no idea why, no one does. The concept makes no real sense to anyone.

This is the room in which she works. A living hell, practically a raging inferno. A circle of hell no one foresaw.

Back and forth with sacks of Coal-two. The sacks are heavy, lumpy, and smell like rot. The room is so hot she often wonders if she might explode.

They have to move fast; they keep busy, focused. They cannot stop.

On occasion, other people, her coworkers, collapse in an exhausted heap. They are carried away by those in black clothing, to the infirmary levels, she supposes.

She wonders if signing the contract for The Destiny was the equivalent of selling her soul to a greedy corporation with a heart of sin.

No one really speaks, yet they regard each other as family. Each person finds survival easier if they escape inside their own minds. Sometimes, someone sings a solitary heart-wrenching tune, the pain and sorrow can be clearly heard. On occasion, Lucy joins in, and once, she sang *Ring-o-ring-o-rosies*, or at least, a little of it. Most of the lyrics are long forgotten to her. Different songs are the only change that occurs.

Every day is the same.

But she is wrong. Today is very different.

On this day, a tall man dressed entirely in black taps her hard on the shoulder.

"Number Sixty-two?" He asks her.

His voice is gruff, and he stands imposing, wary of his surroundings and on high alert.

He shouldn't worry, beady camera eyes are everywhere, and no one would dare hurt him.

Lucy nods. Number Sixty-two is here given number, and she is not supposed to speak to those above her. She knows enough that those in black are a security force, perhaps former military. They cover their faces and carry multiple, vicious weapons. Sometimes, they take people. Those people do not return.

Immediately, she wonders what she's done wrong.

She meets her target every single day; she has to. On rare occasions, she *has* missed her goal by minutes, but the others stepped forward to help. She, in turn, helps them if they fall short. Their job is the most vital one on the ship, after all. They are constantly told such words.

Do they know I miss my targets? Have they been watching me?

"Come with me," the man tells her. "Now," he adds with a growl.

She has no choice.

Briefly, a few of the workers pause to watch her leave. She sees sympathy in their eyes. Misery and sadness. One man even reaches for her, but drops his hand and lowers his head.

Her stomach plummets.

"Am I…" she says and closes her mouth. There are rules.

Sleep, vitamins, work, silence, obey, repeat.

The man pushes her forward as if she has forgotten how to walk and steps behind her. She longs to run but knows she can't, she mustn't. Out of the worker rooms, along a dimly lit metallic corridor until they arrive at a lift.

She has never ventured this far. It isn't allowed.

The rest of the ship is off-limits. She knows there must be multiple layers, all full of workers just like her. Ants in a flying nest, bees in a hive.

"Move," the man orders.

She steps into the lift and tries to think.

If she's done something wrong, she will be leaving out of the airlock. She will die immediately, she hopes.

Her frozen body might wander in space for an eternity. Perhaps she will bounce off the edge of the universe and come spiraling back.

The man presses level forty-two, the upper decks.

The lift travels swiftly. She can barely feel it moving. There is no time to prepare herself. The events are happening too quickly.

When the door opens, she faces a different world entirely. It is the very last sight she expects.

She steps out onto a plush carpet. Deep red with flecks of white. There is soft music playing, gentle songs designed to relax a person. From hell into heaven.

She feels unreal as if she stepped into a wild fantasy. The feeling disorientates her.

A huge sign tells her she is in the *'Upper deck- Kitchen quarters.'*

She can smell food. Delicious mouth-watering real food. She swallows loudly, feeling both shocked and nervous.

"Number Eight," a woman says as she appears from a doorway. "I'll take her."

The man in black grunts, turns and disappears back into the lift.

He's a number too.

"What's your name?" The woman asks her. She is dressed in a one-piece suit of bright blue and looks quite beautiful. Her hair is knotted into a complicated twist. Her skin is smooth and vibrant.

"Sixty-two," she says. The use of her own voice feels strange.

"No, no, your real name."

"Oh. Lucy."

This has to be a dream. This isn't real.

"HIVE picked you as a possible replacement in the kitchen. You've cooked before?"

Lucy knows HIVE is the integrated computer system that is responsible for all life on board.

"Yes."

She worked in one of the popular underground restaurants as a trainee chef before she was selected for the ship. It was a job she hated but still carried out to the best of her abilities.

"Good. We're a chef down and I need you to take his place. You'll be on level forty-two from today. This is a rare opportunity, so don't blow it. Now, follow me."

Lucy, conditioned to do as she is told, follows.

Obey, obey.

Her first step forward catches her off balance. The carpet is too soft under her feet, the sensation feels odd and bouncy.

Get a grip! She warns herself.

The two take several turns until a single door slides open.

"These are your quarters."

There is a large room with four beds. Actual beds with pillows, mattresses, and not hammocks. The bed looks soft and inviting.

The walls are cream with streaks of blue, and nothing looks metallic. The new colors shock her eyes.

"You'll have eight hours of downtime per day and two meals. Understood?"

Eight whole hours!

Lucy feels a ripple of surprise.

"Vitamins too?" She asks.

"No. Not here. That's only for *the below*."

The woman says the last word with great distaste. She behaves as if the three syllables taste bitter or sour inside her pretty mouth.

Lucy hardly notices. She has not eaten real food since they left Earth. Her own taste buds begin to tingle in anticipation. Her mind replays the woman's words.

Wait, only for the below?

A curious sensation flares in her mind. Disbelief and cold horror erupt inside her.

They told us everyone has vitamins?

"But…"

"You have one day off per week, which for you, is today. You'll start tomorrow. New clothing is in that drawer, as are the rules. Good luck."

The woman points her to a bed and leaves. Lucy feels a weight of shock and gratitude. She feels as if she cannot stand and sits straight down on the bed that is now her own.

The change is too great.

The shock of the sudden climb upwards feels so high she might become ill with elevation sickness.

She cannot believe she is where she is. It feels as if she has won some kind of lottery, which she supposes she has in a way.

She pinches herself, in case she fell asleep and is currently dreaming. She feels the pain; she is awake.

She sits on the bed and laughs. She laughs so hard her stomach begins to hurt.

Until one sudden thought hits her and her wild giggling becomes painful tears.

My friends! What about my friends? Why are they treated so differently?

And what about the promise of equality? The main reason she applied in the first place. For her, joining the crew was never about survival. She applied because she wanted to see humanity become the very best it could be.

It is all a lie. Equality, the promised paradise, does not and likely will not ever exist.

The realization sends a shock wave of panic through her body.

The fresh start, the blissful change in humanity, was meant to start on the ship.

Humanity never learns.

While she sits in heaven, her friends, her comrades are still trapped below.

Circles of hell. A futuristic version.

For three days, she empties her mind and smiles at her good fortune. Life for her is better than her wildest dreams were ever able to conjure.

She enjoys sleeping double the time she was used to. The food she eats tastes wonderful. Delicious fresh meat and real vegetables. Her body stops hurting. She no longer feels drained and half insane. Every day is different.

The meals she helps to make are extravagant; artistic in design, and she helps create several courses. The food is of excellent quality, the very best.

Lucy learns quickly. She is allowed to speak if absolutely necessary, but not ask questions. Instead, she listens.

The great space vessel The Destiny has many levels. A pyramid ship.

Command sits at the very top. They have spacious rooms without sharing. They are considered important, essential. Special and superior. They are allowed to shower in real water.

Engineers, scientists, and medical are next. The lifeblood of the ship, the true vital organs.

Next are the elite levels. VIP rooms containing the wealthy, the politicians, and their families. Those levels are vast, spacious and one level even has a gym and a cinema.

Next, are the people meant to build on their new world. The architects, and the ones with specialist trades.

Second VIP sits underneath. The wealthy that paid eye-watering amounts for their tickets. There are hundreds. All living in luxury and comfort.

Next is kitchens. Underneath is storage, followed by domestic, followed by further storage.

Finally, her previous levels. The below. The disposable ones.

She soon learns the name given to her former residence. Her original groups are considered throwaway people. The lowest of the low. The ones who will build what they are told to build on the new planet. The ones who have to obey.

Citizens. The public. They are the same as they were. Nothing more than a workforce of cattle who is entirely expendable. Numbers only.

She also learned that Coal-two is utterly pointless. There is no need to shuttle it back and forth and burn it in a constant furnace. What it really is, is food waste and human waste, compacted into heavy lumps. It is a sick game designed and rigged to invoke order and compliance. Created purely to keep a large number of humans busy, tired, and under full control.

As soon as Lucy learns this, her skin begins to hiss with fury.

It is a job they believe is essential down in the lower levels, vital. Yet it accomplishes nothing but to prevent people from becoming bored and, therefore, unruly.

The perfect control system. Psychological warfare. With no energy to think or act. Kept in a state of exhaustion and, therefore, utter compliance.

They are sardines in a useless tin can and not a ship of exploration and change at all. A flying city of predictable human behavior, corruption, and lies.

In her hours of rest, Lucy thinks. She is a tiny cog in the largest wheel ever built. What can she do?

She cannot stand alone against injustice, lies, and games of vast manipulation. She cannot cut the strings of the puppet masters by herself.

One word out of line, and she will still meet her ending out in space.

Still, she itches to do something, anything. She cannot settle. She will not swallow such unfairness and smile. She will not become one of them.

How can she act as if life is good and fair while her friends suffer such turmoil? How can she hope for a fresh start when such corruption exists on the ship?

***

"Don't put spice on that steak, you fool!"

She hears the head chef yelling. He is a difficult, arrogant man from a privileged and wealthy background. He likes to shout at everyone he can, every chance he gets. He once sat at the Commander's dinner table, and everyone hears the story daily. He hand delivers her food on a silver pretty tray and considers the chore an honor. He behaves as if the woman in charge is the queen of the hive, which Lucy supposes, she truly is.

"She is allergic to spice!" He adds as he throws his tantrum.

The rubbish bin gets to eat the steak.

Several thousand meals are prepared every day. There is so much waste that Lucy threw up when she saw it.

If people were careful, there would be more than enough food for everyone. But no, the disposable are given vitamins instead. A cheaper, cost-effective way and likely drugged with sedatives of some kind too.

"You there!" The wild chef points to Lucy. "Come here now."

She does and just like that, the stars arrange themselves in formation and fate begins to collide.

"Fetch me fresh meat. Now, go! The best piece, do you hear? The best!"

She nods once to show she understands.

Yet she does not know where to go for such a thing. To a freezer unit, she assumes. There must be one so vast that she might find herself lost.

She weaves her way through the large kitchen. Steam and different flavors assault her senses until she's out.

She stands looking for a sign to point the way. The hallways are maze-like in design. A deliberate attempt to confuse or intimidate.

The tall man in black, the gruff speaking one, Number Eight, approaches her.

"Why are you out here?" He demands to know.

"I need to fetch meat."

"Are you authorized?"

"Yes," she lies. "I've been before."

He looks her up and down once and narrows his eyes. She is dressed the part, and she believes she must look harmless enough.

"Follow me," he grunts.

She does. The man walks quite gracefully and swings his hips as he moves. A swagger. A show of authority. A fancy peacock dressed in black.

She follows him down long endless corridors until a plain lift comes into view.

Only those in black can operate them as far as she can tell; the head chef too. They each carry a card for special access to restricted places she cannot go.

Flirt with him, find out how everything works.

"What's your name?" She asks as they step into the lift.

"Eight."

"I mean, your real name."

He turns his head and stares at her. She can only see his suspicious and cruel eyes. Blue ones, like tiny marbles.

"Eight," he repeats. Louder this time. He looks down on her and views her as beneath him.

"Oh."

Asshole.

The lift moves. She can't tell if it goes up or down. There is only a slight jolt as it stops.

The door opens and reveals a blue-colored corridor. She can immediately feel the bitter cold wrap around her body. Her breath is icy.

All this for freezer units?

She feels sickened. She is constantly thinking of her friends on the lower levels, all squeezed into tiny rooms. How can anyone let such a disparity happen?

But she knows that of course they can, after all, it's happened on Earth for many centuries, likely since the dawn of humanity. Tiers of human beings.

"I need a fresh steak," she says.

"Then go. You're trouble," he says. "I know it."

She shakes her head rapidly.

"I'm no one," she answers. She tries to sound meek and fails. Her voice carries the defiance she feels.

She walks forward, knowing she is on a fast-traveling ship on a level with no one she can trust or even talk to.

She is more alone now than when she lived underground in isolation.

Several doors remain closed on either side of her, each one has a sign that states *'Damaged compartment.'*

She guesses the asteroid storm the ship flew through caused serious issues.

Come on, come on, where am I going?

As soon as one door opens, she steps inside as if the room was her true aim all along.

If she expected to see hanging animal carcasses, she was wrong. If she expected to see wall-to-wall freezer units containing lab-created meats, she was wrong.

People.

Human beings are hanging from hooks built into the ceiling.

Some, she even recognizes.

It takes everything she has not to fall apart right there. Her sanity shudders in revulsion. Shock makes her jolt wildly.

She staggers back, appalled and horrified. She retches loudly.

Why, how, who? Questions collide with force. She drops to her knees and immediately feels the chill of the room engulf her body.

It can't be possible. It just can't.

Why would people be eaten? Meat is grown in a lab and has been for many years. Animals only exist in exotic zoos or in a DNA bank, ready to be born again on a new world.

Count to five. You're imagining this. One, two, three, four…

She cannot resist a second look. A peer closer. She is witnessing the truth, not an illusion or some wild hallucination. The visions are not trapped inside her own mind.

Some bodies appear to have been used. Chunks of thighs are missing, sliced away by expert knives. Buttocks too. One body has been stripped entirely. The innards are missing. The chest cavity is wide open. Barely a skeleton left hanging.

"Hurry up," the man outside yells.

Lucy stands and tries to control her shaking body. She swallows the burn of vomit.

He cannot know that she did not know.

She has to act naturally. As if running into cannibalized human bodies is an everyday occurrence.

"Okay," she shouts back.

The emotion and revulsion in her tones give her away. She glances around the long room. There must be a hundred or more people hanging.

Metal drawers with a layer of ice line the edges of the vast room.

She scrambles over and pulls at one. A label on an airtight bag says pork. Lucy thinks that might be a lie. She yanks at several other compartments until the word steak jumps out at her.

A tear snakes its way down her face and freezes.

Act naturally. Act normally.

"What's taking so long?"

She takes three deep breaths and smiles. Her lips crack in protest. She races across the room and out of the door.

She must lie. She must be calm.

"I was choosing the best," she says, far too brightly. "For her, the Commander."

Her heart is in her throat. She blinks rapidly, her vision is distorted.

Inside, she screams until she is raw.

A gun gets poked into her spine until she finds herself moving, back to the lift, back to the kitchen, back into chaos and madness.

***

Eight hours of downtime.

She does not sleep. Instead, she lies awake staring at the ceiling and wondering what became of humanity. She thinks of all those above her and, of course, those below.

Decadence? Gluttony? Seven sins and more contained within a flying vessel.

As Earth died, people still expected the finer things in life. She knows this. The death of their own planet was nothing more than an inconvenience to some. They still wished to dance, spend, hold lavish parties and invoke jealousy in others for the sake of vanity and ego.

Greed and inequality would die alongside earth, or so the elite leaders and politicians promised and swore.

Pacts were made and documents were signed. Hands were shaken and wars were halted.

Equality would be the new way of life in the promised land. Democracy and fairness. Sharing would live inside the human heart in place of hate. Lessons had been learned, they claimed, and capitalism would die.

Lies.

Pretty gift-wrapped lies, but false words all the same.

The fault of the leaders. Those who were voted in unfairly or those with a mythical special bloodline that allegedly makes them superior in nature and with a genetic right to rule. Blue bloods. Predisposed to disgrace.

Lucy sits up and looks at those around her. Her three roommates are sleeping without guilt or conscience nagging them awake. There is never sympathy in their eyes, no regret or disgust, and they must know. Not a day passes when someone isn't sent for fresh goods from the freezers.

Have I eaten that meat?

It is a question that has haunted her every minute since her terrible discovery. She does not dare answer her own thoughts.

She wonders if perhaps she should throw herself out of the airlock. She wants no place in the new world, simply because it is not new at all. The hope she had died inside her the moment she was removed from below and understood the truth.

She sobs loudly and clamps a hand over her mouth.

"What's wrong?"

The voice comes to her in the darkness. It is the voice of Melody, a calm and quiet woman, and the head chef's current favorite toy.

Lucy does not answer. Cannot. To speak the words she thinks out loud is to invite death.

The cold-hearted ones, those in black, will arrive and kill her. She, too, will be eaten by greedy mouths and sliced by fine silver cutlery.

I don't care. I don't care anymore. I can't do this.

"I said, what's wrong?"

An explosion occurs inside. She cannot hold the darkness at bay.

"Freezer," she hisses, without really meaning to.

One loaded word, full of meaning.

"Oh. Didn't you know?"

"No," she admits. "No one below knows."

"Bathroom. Ten minutes. Quietly."

Is this a trap?

Melody stands and stretches. She exaggerates her movements and presses the door to open.

Lucy sits and considers her options. Melody clearly knows things she does not. Knowledge is a powerful tool. But so is betrayal. The only people she feels she can trust live on the lower levels, the below.

Right now, they will be working hard while I rest. Are all those who collapse eaten?

Thinking such a thing makes her brain untether further.

Half of her feels that she should forget what she saw and enjoy her new existence. The three years will pass much faster and easier if she keeps her head down and her mouth shut.

Life on the new planet might work? People truly can change.

Her heart tells her otherwise.

She waits the allotted time and stands. It is a risk, a gamble to know the truth, but she needs it.

"Remember the asteroid hit? That huge impact? Vital parts broke. There was a fire too. Storage was ruined badly. It was a month or so after we left, and nothing could be fixed. There was no choice. Over a quarter of the supplies were lost. Now there isn't enough left, nor enough vitamins for everyone for the whole journey either. That's what I heard. We'll starve without doing this. Everyone says so."

Lucy considers Melody's cold words. There is no emotion in her tone, only a quiet acceptance. Clearly, she had made peace with such murder and brutality.

The wall dividing the cubicle stands between them, a barrier separating opposing views.

"Do those above know what, no, who they're eating?" She asks.

"Yes, they all made the decision, a vote. All of the people in charge and the passengers, they're used to the very best food. The best of everything. People war or fight when they're hungry. They rebel against authority. The commander said so. Another chef, he stood up against it all and..."

Lucy feels her stomach flip. Is that whose place she took? The one who took a stand?

"Did he go out of the airlock?"

"No, no one does, really. That's just what they say as a threat of punishment. He went to the freezer."

At this, she retches.

"Shh, stop it! If they know we're talking in here, it's over. Just keep your head down and blend in. It's the only way."

"It's wrong! It's so wrong, don't you see that?"

"Yes, but what can we do? Nothing. Look, we've only got three years of this. Only three. I'm sorry, but we've got to survive. Our whole species is at stake."

Only three years! I can't.

"Life will be different on the new planet," Melody adds. "It really will. We can forget all about what happened on this ship. That's why those in black cover their faces. So no one knows who they are. They won't face retribution for the things they do now."

That isn't true. For as long as she lives, she will recognize the callous and cold eyes of Number Eight.

"We could ration," she pleads.

"They won't do that! Most people paid everything they had for this trip, they paid to survive! They want the best. They think this is a long holiday! Or a cruise ship. I've got to go. We'll look suspicious."

"Wait," Lucy whispers. "Why did you choose to tell me?"

"Because I get it, I came from the below too."

Melody opens her cubicle door with a loud squeak. She washes her hands and leaves without saying another word.

She sits on the cold metallic toilet and puts her head in her hands. What if Melody is right? Maybe survival really is in doubt? It might be a case of do or die.

Perhaps she should keep her head down and wait for time to pass. It works for Melody, after all.

She thinks of all the hard work down in the below, the pointless job everyone works so hard on. They all think it's so important and it's utterly meaningless.

The only value they have is for food. Human cattle, branded by numbers.

No. It has to stop. It can't be allowed. Being human means having respect for other humans. It does not mean feasting on the bones and flesh of her own dead friends. Perhaps under desperate circumstances, the act of eating human flesh would be less vile. Yet those above are not starving or desperate. They hold parties and wild events. They do not suffer. They waste what they have.

They lounge in decadence and greed.

She has to do something, or she will be as far away from human as they are.

Precious information has been given to her for a reason, or so she believes. She cannot stand by and do nothing.

***

Day after day passes.

She has no opportunities, no chance at saving those below her. As she helps create intricate meals in the busy kitchens, she thinks and tries to plot.

There is no way she can organize a rebellion and demand change. She cannot access higher levels and she knows those around her won't join her efforts.

The VIP levels and upwards are heavily guarded by those in black. She wonders if poison might be accessible. Perhaps something stolen from domestic, a cleaning fluid to place in the food, perhaps.

This too, she knows, would likely be impossible. Besides, what is the point in murdering to prevent murder?

She knows that those in charge watch them all closely. The below people are their source of entertainment.

She heard a rumor, several of them, that life in the below is streamed on large screens for the amusement of the elite. They laugh at the daily suffering and place bets on who might fall from exhaustion.

There were always stories on Earth of a hidden government cabal, designed to secretly run the world. She always disregarded such talk, yet now she wonders if a secret group might truly run life on the ship. It can't just be the Commander making decisions. Others agreed to the eating of human flesh.

Lucy has visited the remaining freezer storage rooms. They are so vast that they seem more like massive warehouses. Each room is packed to the ceiling with viable food.

Fresh vegetables are also grown in the hydro labs. She is no mathematician, but she knows enough about calculations to understand that there is enough to go around, more than enough if they abandoned greed.

Their new planet is said to hold all manner of wild animals and edible foods, so it's not as if anything has to be saved.

She feels a sharp elbow in her ribs and gasps. Melody is at her side.

"Are you better now?" She whispers.

Lucy glances around, certain many eyes are watching her, but no one is. They are all lost in their own tasks. She nods and shrugs.

"There's nothing I can do, no matter what I think," she answers.

She continues chopping vegetables, the slow rhythm helps to calm her frantic mind.

"It will be different," Melody says. "When we get there."

"No, it won't. We both know that."

She knows she speaks the truth. The disparity between humanity has always been present, just like war and violence. One person alone might exist in a neutral state, two might exist in happiness. Three and conflict arrives. One gets pushed out. More than three and groups begin to form. One group decides they want what the others have and begin a war, and so on.

The entire construct is as pyramid-shaped as The Destiny is.

War and conflict have never ceased on their old planet. From the beginning of recorded history, people were kept in slavery to serve their gods and special rulers or sent to fight for the ownership of other nations. They must build and kneel at the feet of those above.

Even at the end of everything on Earth, places to live underground were of great value. Anyone without good health or money, a job or skill, was left to die on the surface and there were a great many who perished. Huge doors were slammed in the faces of children, in the faces of the old and desperate, without a shred of remorse.

Of course, those in charge were safe.

Lucy had been born into life underground. The surface for her only existed in picture books and old photographs.

Free will has always been a falsehood.

Control the masses and give them the gift of illusion. The illusion of freedom and self-ownership.

A simple rule that never fails and if that rule should begin to crumble. Start a war. Divide and conquer.

She wonders how long it might take until groups form and separate on their new planet? Of course, war will follow.

Who will they send to fight in their elaborate chess games?

The people from below. The disposable ones.

The expendable workforce given numbers and not names, forced into a conflict that is not their own.

***

Lucy watches and thinks. She waits for opportunity or fate to intercede.

When the head chef begins to smile at her, she smiles back. When he winks and saves her a tiny piece of raspberry pie, she eats it ravenously and acts graciously. When he touches her arm and makes eye contact, she glances back with lies inside her own eyes.

When he invites her to the observation deck that same evening, she accepts with deep gratitude.

A spark of an idea occurs. She has the beginnings of a plan, a thin fuse lights. A countdown begins.

The head chef, Zachary, uses his keycard to access the lift.

She notices the code he presses and remembers. The lift jolts very slightly as it moves. She smiles, unsure of what to say.

"You make excellent pastry," Zachary tells her. "Who taught you?"

For fucks sake!

What a curious thing to say. A compliment on her baking techniques. Zachary is a large man, and not at all pleasant to look at. He sweats and eats enough per day for four people; he has a wild temper, and no one dares to tell him no, including her.

"I worked in Koi, in the main underground city. Under Denver," she answers. "I greatly admire your skills, too."

He nods enthusiastically as the lift stops.

She wonders what she will see when the door opens. More lavish rooms and space for thousands? Well-dressed individuals with all the time in the world and with bellies full of her friends?

She sees neither of those things. She sees a large and empty observation deck with a thick window.

The vision of space fills her eyes.

She never imagined it would look so beautiful.

She gasps loudly and throws a hand up to her mouth.

"It's something, isn't it," Zachary smiles.

Something doesn't even cover it. She steps forward, eager to see more. Child-like wonder fills her. The vision in her eyes is glorious. The most beautiful of all sights.

The ship is traveling faster than she imagined, yet she can see tiny pinpricks of lights being left behind. Vast clouds made of colors she has never seen before hang in space. Close by is a huge planet with lavish swirls of orange. Almost as if someone with an artist flare passed by with a paintbrush and made it to be that way.

All those worlds out there. All those civilizations.

It seems impossible that they should be the only ones. Humanity, jumping from planet to planet and leaving nothing but destruction in their wake. They might be feared and avoided by other races.

She can understand why.

Waves of strong emotion wash over her. The feeling is so great that it feels as if the waves contain enough power to scar her soul.

She is struck by the sudden urge to disable the ship. To destroy it. Halt the plague of humans. Stop the spread of the infection that is people.

She steps forward, as close as she can get. She grips the metallic bars; the coolness numbs her.

The elite on the ship, the ones who put no value on human life, do not deserve such a view. She is willing to bet that they take the sight of the universe for granted, and bets that they take the vision of such eternity as commonplace.

Revolution, she thinks. The single word serves to remind her of her mission. Her goal.

Humanity, with parasitical leaders spreading a vile agenda.

Her stomach plummets as she turns to the arrogant chef. She understands what she must do. There is a quick clarity inside her thoughts.

Every revolution demands a sacrifice, but not a pile of victims. The only blood to be spilled must be her own.

"Thank you, for this I mean," she says and points out towards space.

He has taken her to the observation deck in exchange for sex; she knows this. He is bored of Melody, no doubt. He wants a new toy with which to play.

He smiles, fully expecting that she will feel grateful enough to share his bed for the night. He closes his eyes, ready to receive worship for his greatness or perhaps a kiss, a promise of things to come.

Lucy snatches his keycard in one fierce swipe and runs.

The sandglass that is her life, tips. Time and sand grains are running out and she knows it.

The lit fuse makes its way to the stick of dynamite that is her goal, her end game.

She is back inside the lift before he even begins to yell.

Please work, please work.

Lucy has pinned every single one of her hopes on this moment. If the head chef, greasy, creepy Zachary, delivers food to the Queen Bee Commander himself, chances are, his keycard will take her to the engineering level at least.

The beating heart of the ship, the essential valve. The location of HIVE.

The card beeps in solidarity and flashes green, she presses the remembered code and feels the lift move.

Her legs almost give out from underneath her in relief. Her body feels boneless.

This is a suicide mission.

She knows. She understands and accepts the penalty. She has seen the beauty of space. The ugliness of the people on board doesn't belong alongside such glory.

The door slides open, and she holds her breath. She expects to see armed guards and multiple guns pointed at her head or those in black waiting to pounce.

Yet the hallway is quiet. A dead zone. Command clearly does not expect a single person to oppose them.

Signs alert her to various departments. She runs past the majority, frantically reading and searching.

It is HIVE she needs, and she needs the room desperately. Its electronic tendrils and functions spread far around the ship, the system has more of a reach than any one person.

To her left is a clear window with a room full of elaborate flashing lights flickering on massive computer units. There. HIVE. Her aim.

One of those in black exits the room just as she tries to enter. Neither one sees the other, and both are taken by surprise as they collide in a tangle. It is the tall one, with the gruff voice. Number Eight. Of course, it had to be him. Fate arranged for the meeting.

"Hey," he yells before he tumbles to the ground. "It's you!"

His eyes widen, and she sees his fury. He will end her.

Lucy takes her chance. In his hands, he holds a weapon. He will raise it to her head within seconds and it will be over before she has even begun.

She is faster. Adrenaline is coursing through her body. She swipes the gun from his holster belt and hits him viciously in the temple.

He falls still. All brawn and no bite. Goodnight, Number Eight.

She crawls away and leaves him in a heap. The room is her goal. She forces herself to her feet and closes the door.

Only a few grains of her life now remain.

Two open-mouthed people dressed in white lab coats face her, wild rabbits caught unawares. Neither one moves, they only stare at her with wide and confused eyes.

"Listen," she gasps. "Do as I say, and no one gets hurt."

She raises her stolen gun and points it. She has no intention of pulling the trigger.

Think. Be calm. Be strong.

She has minutes, maybe even seconds.

"I want the lift doors on the lower levels opened. And access to all levels. Every door, do you understand me?"

"We can't," the small woman's voice shakes as she answers. Lucy knows her words must be false. HIVE can do anything, that's what it was created for, its whole purpose.

"I'll kill you where you stand, I swear it. I want to speak to them too. Those below."

"This is outrageous!"

How long will it take for creepy Zachary to alert someone? How long might it take before she is found?

They will be searching for her, hunting her down. They might even guess where she is.

"I have a bomb. It will detonate unless you do as I ask," she lies.

She cannot hear any alarm sounds. There are no loud and angry voices barreling towards her, not yet.

"No," the man snaps. "We won't. You're a terrorist!"

Hypocrisy is rife.

Shit, shit, shit!

"Whoever can do what I ask, do it now. The other gets a bullet. Five, four, three…"

"All right, all right. Just don't detonate, please."

The small woman sits at the computer station and begins to type rapidly. Her fingertips sound like heavy falling rain. She is frowning and tutting. Twice, she swipes her own card, to access the mainframe, Lucy supposes.

She is taking too long.

A screen in front of her flashes *EMERGENCY RELEASE. Y, N.*

"Don't do this," the man says. "Please."

Lucy ignores him. She must do it.

"You can speak now," the woman says as she jabs the Y button. "I can record it."

She is no fool. She knows full well that such a recording will never be heard by the ears it is meant for.

"No, that won't do. It has to be live."

More relentless tapping. Above her head, the lights begin to dim and flash.

They're coming. They're coming now.

"Can this door be locked?" She shouts.

"You wanted them all open! So no."

A flaw in her plan. An obvious one she hadn't once foreseen.

"Hurry then," she yells.

The man moves. He intends to run away and shout for help; she knows this. She pulls the trigger of her gun and watches as he crumples to the ground and folds himself up. Blood immediately pools around him.

She hit his thigh; she thinks. It won't be fatal. Only a wound meant to slow and not stop a person. She is not a killer. She is not like those she seeks to ruin.

His wild screaming overtakes all other sounds.

"Oh my God," the woman gasps.

"You're next if you don't do as I ask."

More sounds of furious tapping.

"You can speak now," the woman says and darts away. She does not help her coworker; she flees into a corner and hides under a desk instead.

What if she's lying?

There is no other choice but to trust her word. A thing she hates to do. The ones above her are complicit. Guilt by association, by agreement.

The screen insists she has replaced the machine-like voice in lower levels, the same voice that counts down and the one she hated so very much.

"This is Lucy," she says with practiced words. Time and time again, she had written a speech inside her mind. Words that might rouse and wake the people she worked alongside.

"I'm number sixty-two. I worked with you. You're all being lied to. Coal-two is food waste, it's fake. It's a control system for keeping order. Please listen... I..."

Loud voices erupt and come closer all too quickly. The shot man falls silent.

"They're eating you. They're eating your bodies. They watch and laugh. The freezers. It was all lies. You're expendable. The VIPs, the elites, there's plenty of food. You must rise up. You must. The doors and lifts are open. Run. Overtake the ship. Save yourselves. It was all a trick. Remember me. It was all a..."

The door bursts open.

Those in black fill the room. Number Eight is back on his feet and his eyes are savage. She drops her stolen gun.

It was worth it.

"Listen," Lucy begs. "Stop this. We can..."

He punches her in the face and down she goes into blackness and oblivion.

Now

Number Eight stares down at the woman's body. He is glad he got to be the one to kill her, the one to pull the trigger. It was a gift, a pleasure. He is not pleased she died laughing. Why was she not afraid? Even now her heartbeat has stopped, she smiles in death as if mocking him.

He wonders if he should have made her suffer. She might not be at peace then.

After all, she killed an unarmed man.

The blaring alarms sound far too loud. The lights flash and make him feel disorientated.

His head throbs with pain. She really hit him hard and with his own gun, of all things.

"Stupid bitch," he mutters.

He knew she was trouble. He could sense something off about her. Why didn't anyone listen to him? Now look, she's caused so much trouble.

Close to his feet, the injured man in the white lab coat moves. Oh, she hasn't killed him after all.

"Eight, come on, we need to patrol," one of his coworkers shouts. "Check it's all clear."

"Shouldn't we take her to the freezer while she's fresh?" He answers. "And him to the infirmary?"

"Yeah, we probably…"

Gunfire erupts.

Number Eight, whose real name is Colin Harold Smith, is immediately rattled. Gunfire rarely happens onboard the ship. Bullets are only reserved for those who step out of line.

More gunfire noises. Followed by the gut-wrenching sounds of screams.

What could have happened? She only spoke to those kept in the below.

"She wanted the doors open," a woman's voice says. "She said she had a bomb."

Colin squints and sees her. A small figure in white is tucked under a desk.

"She did what?" He gasps.

"The doors and lifts. They're open."

"Which ones?"

"All of them."

"Fuck!"

"Yeah, fuck."

Now what? And a bomb? What the hell are they supposed to do?

Security is meant to be an easy job. Law and order. He only has to keep law and order.

If those from below are coming up. There's going to be a massacre.

"RUN!" He hears a third man in black yell. His fast, dark shape passes by the door in a blur.

Run or hide? Run or hide? Colin thinks.

Too late. There is not enough time to decide.

A quick peek out of the door informs him that a large mob is sprinting up the plush hallway. He does not have enough bullets to take them all down.

They are not just a mob; they run with fierce and brutal intent, muscles fueled by revenge. At least thirty people. He can only stare, open-mouthed. The group is strong, likely from constant work. They are enraged. He can smell their anger and disgust.

He will not win against such viciousness, such fury.

He does the only thing he can think to do. He drops his gun and raises his hands in surrender.

He cannot die. Not like this. He deserves to live. He isn't like the others. Yes, he treated people badly. He liked the power it gave him, that was all. Yes, he ate the flesh of other human beings, but still… he wanted to start again on the new planet. Terrible crimes could be left behind and forgotten.

He braces for impact and prays to a God no one believes in anymore.

The crowd hits him as one. He stands no chance at all. Instant karma.

Down and down he falls. Booted feet stamp on his head. Fists punch him. The pain is severe and crippling. Agony burst out across his curled-up body.

"I'm sorry," he tries to shout.

A heavy foot sees opportunity in his empty mouth and kicks several of his teeth out.

Those in charge did not create a pliable workforce.

They did not create compliant, docile people. They made an army.

Colin becomes one of the first to die. No one really keeps track.

Mayhem and chaos break out across all levels of The Destiny.

A war within.

Thousands rise against thousands, hundreds fall as the ship calmly speeds towards its destination.

After

The Destiny lands without any major engineering issues.

The new planet is more beautiful than anyone could have dreamed of.

Melody is one of the last to descend the ramps. The sky is blue, just as it used to be on Earth, and the grass is green. Darker than Earth grass once was, but green all the same. A goldilocks planet with the sun in the right position, a lilac-colored sun.

She can see lush forests and serene lakes. There is flat land to build on, with materials still in storage.

Life will be good. It is the promised land, after all, or is it?

She is still in chains.

She feels a shove from behind her and moves her feet to keep rhythm with the human chain. All of the prisoners have to walk as one or they will become tangled in a twisted puzzle of limbs and bodies. The chains that bind them are short.

The war on board was over quickly. It was won by those from the below. Anger is mightier than guilt.

Roles have been reversed. The elite, command, and VIPs became the expendable ones, the discarded, the ones below.

The lone crusader woman Lucy, her plan, although done, some claim, with pure intentions, has backfired in the worst possible way.

The people from the below levels became entranced by decadence and the finer things in life. They came to adore and yearn for everything they never had before. As the food did indeed run out, they were forced to eat those in storage.

Lucy had it wrong, she had everything wrong.

Sometimes those who begin at the bottom, really do forget they ever existed in such a place. They become accustomed, comfortable and they contain a single strong emotion within their hearts.

Revenge.

The strongest desire of all. Forgiveness has fallen short. There is none.

The below became the people they despised and, of course, the elite became the ones they laughed at. Politicians, leaders, the wealthy, became the ones living in tiny rooms and sleeping short hours in hammocks.

Tables turned and flipped entirely.

Her group, one of many, is led forward and onto the new grass. There is no time to enjoy fresh air inside their lungs, no time to stop and give thanks. No time to appreciate or mourn those who didn't make it.

They have to build now. A village, a town, or even a city. They all have twenty-hour workdays and four hours of sleep. Slaves.

They are numbers. They are tired, exhausted.

They are not laughing now.

Change did arrive, polarity switched. Roles reversed.

Humanity itself never truly learns.

UNDER THE EARTH

Alex walks into the small pub with great purpose. She is set to meet five carefully vetted individuals, chosen by herself. Many applied; people always do, and she remains selective in who she picks.

She said no to the mother of three. No to the single father and absolutely not to the young man who claimed he was a carer, looking after his elderly parents.

She makes brief yet essential eye contact with the solitary barman, Vince. He is busy cleaning glasses that are already perfectly spotless.

The pub carries a curious scent. Cheap perfume and forgotten, tired old fantasies.

She stops to smell the bitter air. It feels sorrowful inside the walls, stale, morose, and hollow.

Years of pain and regret have been etched onto the flowery wallpaper and spilled onto the familiar patterned carpet.

Middle-aged men and women sit at the small bar in relative silence, afraid to go home and face their partners or equally afraid to go home and face no one at all.

They each nurse a single drink with tobacco-stained fingertips. Perhaps they think of the past, a time when their lives felt full of endless possibilities instead of the constant doom they now face daily. Or might they think of the future and all the terror it is sure to hold.

No one turns to look at her. They have seen her many times before and couldn't care less what she does or how she does it.

She glances once more at Vince and waits for him to nod his head. He does so quickly, a barely-there jerk. He behaves as if they are undercover spies swapping traitorous information or illicit lovers arranging to meet in code.

They are neither.

She is only borrowing the back room of the pub for fifteen, perhaps twenty minutes. It makes her enterprise feel more professional, meeting in a public place.

She walks across the old sticky carpet; her tough boots make kissing sounds as she steps. Dead inside eyes watch her without interest.

Nothing ever changes inside the pub, or the village, and such a thing works in her favor.

The backroom has a door labeled '*THE SNUG.*'

The sign is a lie. There is nothing snug or nice about the room. It is small, cold, damp, and has mold growing rapidly in each corner. Decay and rot are always present.

She knocks lightly on the door and plasters a smile on her face, it is time to appear confident. She has an important job to do, and she must do it right. She is dressed in a waterproof jacket, thick jeans, and heavy boots. A no-nonsense outfit.

The door swings open and she sees her five chosen people in flesh, blood, and bone. Not the pixelated images she knows.

Eager expressions peer at her. Five people willing and paying to put their complete trust in her.

She knows each one more than they could ever imagine she might. In the modern age, it is easy to find information about everyone. There are no secrets, not when the internet is involved, and people share their lives so freely.

Adam, Kerry, Max, Jack, and Asif.

A quick glance and she already knows who is who.

Still, it is important she keeps up appearances.

"Hi," she smiles. "I'm Alex. Thank you for coming."

She steps forward and makes a show of shaking hands while introductions are done.

"And you are?" She repeats to each person.

No one senses her deceit.

She perches on the smallest stool in the room. It is already growing dark outside; she needs only minutes to run through her safety advice.

She lowers her voice and eases forward. The rest follow suit and mimic her.

"Do you all have the cash payments as requested?" She asks.

She charges one hundred pounds per person.

The five nod their heads in curious synchronicity, rifle in their pockets, and hand envelopes over.

"Thanks, that's great. We'll use my van to drive to the location. Once there, you *will* need to follow my rules. I must be ahead of you at all times. You must keep sight of each other. You cannot take your phones down with you."

"What! Why?" The girl called Kerry whines.

She shakes her blonde head rapidly and pouts.

Alex already knows she is the dramatic type. The one that will complain the loudest and scream over every small noise or slight hazard they encounter. She can tell.

"What we're doing," Alex reminds them. "Is illegal. Essentially, we'll be trespassing on government land. Phones have to be off when we leave here, and I mean it. Keep them off and in my van, or they might ping the phone towers. Nobody, especially the police, can know we're out there. If you don't agree, say so now and leave."

Sometimes, it is better that she behaves with strict authority.

"That's fine," Adam announces. "We'll follow your rules."

He is the boyfriend of Kerry. The two have been together for one year and four months. They enjoy, or rather, he enjoys hiking and sailing. They regularly post photos and tag each other into the images they take.

It is easy to find a person's hobby on social media, which is why Alex never uses it. Unless she's spying on others or advertising her private tours.

"What if we get into trouble down there?" Asif asks. "Or one of us gets injured?"

He is the one she needs to watch the most. He is sharp and clever and already has narrowed, suspicious eyes aimed her way.

"I have an emergency radio," she lies. "With a beacon, one that works underground, and don't worry, we'll be fine. Think of this as a once-in-a-lifetime adventure. Which is what you all booked me for."

"How many groups have you taken down there?" The man called Jack asks.

Jack and Asif are a couple. They live together and have a fish tank full of exotic and colorful fish. They too enjoy hiking and skiing. Jack likes to cook intricate meals while Asif finds pleasure in listening to Mozart and drinking expensive wine.

"Ten groups so far," she answers. "This is a fairly new venture. I'm the only person who knows the route, so please, no remembering or map-drawing."

"How did you find it?" Max asks.

He is the lone member of the group. A solo man. He lives alone too. He takes photographs of sunsets and posts uplifting quotes. He has a beard with streaks of gray swirling around inside. He claims to meditate daily and seems to enjoy funny cat memes the best.

He climbed a mountain once, but Alex forgets which one. It looked fiercely big and cold, wherever it was.

"I was exploring the area," she says. "And I fell."

She speaks the truth, in a way. She did indeed fall into the place she leads the tours.

"What happened?" Max asks.

"Another time, we have to leave now. It's dark enough. Follow me."

Little ducklings all in a row: follow her, they do.

***

The drive isn't a long one. All the same, she takes a needlessly spiraling route in order to confuse them, just in case. She hopes they all find it harder to recall and lose their sense of direction. One can never be too careful.

Her van seats six people. Her five whisper excitedly among themselves behind her seat. There is much to look forward to.

Rural exploration inside a lost and forgotten underground network.

That's what she advertises her tour as. The statement is not a lie. There are many miles to explore. Old and forgotten military bunkers hold vast secrets, as do solid Victorian sewer systems and natural underground chambers. Forgotten and abandoned mines, too. They branch off like honeycombs under everyone's feet.

No one ever stops to wonder what secrets and old history exist underfoot. In fact, no one ever stops to wonder about anything anymore.

She sees a familiar old sign half hanging from a rusty barbed wire fence.

It's almost time.

"Under your seats," Alex half yells to her group. "Are hard hats. Please put them on now. But not the headlamps until I say so."

She hears the swish-sounding movements of clothing. Each person is rummaging and mumbling to themselves and each other.

She turns off her van's headlights and slows down. The isolated track can be treacherous, even more so without decent light.

She only has the moon to lend a glow, and it isn't enough to see without straining.

The people behind her fall quiet. They are nervous now. No doubt having last-minute regrets.

Sometimes in life, those who go seeking adventure and flirting with danger find what it is they are looking for. The exhilaration of staring death in the face, only to remain alive, fuels them further. Or the adrenaline a close shave with fatality brings only inspires more illicit thrills, with greater risks each time.

She understands the needs of the group. In another life, she might have been one of them.

"Hold on, this is a bumpy track," she calls out.

Her van grinds and jerks in protest as she drives over potholes and dips. She makes a sharp left turn into an almost invisible clearing, and stops when the van is nestled behind bushes and trees.

"Do we…" A voice says.

"Shhh," she cuts them off. "Wait."

A barbed-wire fence with a wide cut open hole faces them. There is only a lone field ahead unless a person knows the secret the ground holds. Yet she is looking for lights.

On occasion, she has wandered into dog walkers and once, a couple on a blanket making love under a full moon. They were not from her village, and that presented problems. Police too, sometimes officers patrol on foot or search the nearby woodland, for what or who, she can only guess.

"Okay, leave your phones behind. Keep your lights off and follow me. We'll take a selfie afterward, for your social media."

She stuffs her envelopes full of money into her glove box. Her van will be safe. The surrounding trees on the border of the woods offer enough shelter and darkness. Come daylight, she will be long gone.

It has rained for the last few days. The grassy field remembers and holds the water greedily, unwilling to let a single drop leave. She instructed everyone to wear appropriate clothing and boots, so nobody finds such a muddy mess a difficult issue.

Alex counts her steps inside her mind. She stops at exactly step number forty-two.

She switches her headlight on and waits for the group to assemble around her.

They form a cluster, peering with wide and excited eyes.

She rolls back a large piece of carefully positioned turf and reveals a wide metal hatch that looks quite like a sewer entrance. Tendrils of branch and vine grow from the ground and help with concealment.

"This," she begins. She always tells the same story and not once does it lose its charm. She taps the ground with her steel-toed boot. The sound of the metal reverberates.

"This was the entrance to a former, highly secret military bunker. Originally, there were underground compartments for sheltering select people in an emergency. What the builders did not know was that the area was already hollowed in places by a mining operation and by nature herself. The collapse of a single wall revealed chambers. The chambers and passages link up to an abandoned underground train station that was never fully finished or used. You are about to explore a place few people will ever see. You are privileged. Truly. Now, I expect it won't be long before the area is re-discovered officially and sealed. You might well be the last group I can take down there."

"And it's safe?" Kerry questions her. "I mean, are you certain you can get us out if we trip or break a leg or…"

"Yes, I can."

"Does anyone else know where we'll be? I mean, what if you fall and…"

"Yes, my business partner knows when we're due out," Alex answers.

"But we don't even know you and I… I think I've changed my mind. This feels really off. I'm sorry."

The girl has more of a powerful instinct than Alex guessed.

She feels her heart stutter and jerk. There's always one. She can't beg or plead. It's far too obvious. Instead, she knows she will have to act with indifference. Reverse psychology almost. She swallows her panic.

"Your loss," she says. "But this is a safe tour."

The group is silent; she wonders if they will follow Kerry like lemmings. Once a seed of doubt is planted inside imagination, it can be hard to crush such a force.

"Well, I for one can't wait," Max says. He pulls at his beard and tucks it away under his jacket. "I'll go first if you like," he adds. "I've been spelunking. I know how dark it'll be."

Alex brushes dirt from the metal hatch and listens hard. She catches every word of Adam and Kerry's whispered conversation as he pulls her away for privacy. Sound carries easily.

Kerry is whining like a trapped cat.

"Come on, you promised," Adam says. "Please, don't let me down. I so want to do this and when we get back, imagine how cool we'll look on Facebook and Insta! Imagine how many likes we'll get."

"But Adam…"

"It's all safe and professional. You heard her, and she has a website!"

Come on, Alex thinks. Persuade her.

Asif crouches down and leans forward, one eyebrow raised.

"I didn't know there were any old underground stations and bunkers out here. I thought that was just in London," he says.

He doesn't sound suspicious or accusing, only curious, and his voice is full of wonder.

"Secret bases. *Secret* is the keyword here," Alex tells him and winks.

"Got it," he grins.

"All right," Adam says. "We're in. We'll come down."

Yes!

No doubt, the opportunity to boast on social media was very persuasive.

"I'll open the hatch and follow you down, Max, as you offered to go first. Please feel free and yes, it will be dark."

It's hard for her to see his expression in such blackness, but she imagines he is smiling proudly. He has been picked first, likely a thing that doesn't happen to him very often.

She grips the outer handle of the hatch and yanks it with all her strength. The metal grinds loudly and creaks as it opens.

"Lights on," she gasps with effort.

Multiple lights shine and hit her in the face.

Max leans forward and sees a ladder fixed against one wall. The hatch is wide, with plenty of space. Still, it isn't a hole claustrophobic people should ever tackle.

He arranges his footing and climbs down. Each person can hear the echoing clang of his boots on metal as he goes.

"It's not a long climb down, only eight rungs," Alex reassures the rest. As if on cue, Max calls out.

"Made it!"

Asif goes next, followed by Jack.

Alex wonders if Kerry might make a run for it and dart across the field and away.

She surprises her and takes a single deep breath before she, too, rolls her eyes and climbs down.

Finally, Adam follows.

Alex takes a moment to look up at the night sky. All she can see of the universe is tiny pinpricks of light like campfire flames sparkling against night eternal.

Life, truly, it must exist in huge quantities out there and here she is, crawling around in a muddy field and wandering forbidden places with deceit in her heart and emptiness where her soul should sit.

Still, any alternative she doesn't bear thinking about. She does what she does for a reason.

"Alex? Are you there?" Asif shouts. There is a slight waver in his voice. Worry. Do they all expect her to slam the hatch down and leave?

"Coming," she answers.

One last thing to do.

She gazes across the field, searching the tree line of the thick woods. She flicks her headlamp off and on twice. A distant torchlight follows suit and does the same. She knows the meaning; she is good to go, there are no outsiders around.

Communication via signals of light.

She drops down onto the first rung and pulls the hatch shut behind her.

✳✳✳

Blackness. Chaos. Disorder. Malevolence. Bleakness. The underworld, no Hades present.

"What's that horrible smell?"

It is Kerry who speaks first.

As Alex lets her eyes adjust, all she can see are blobs of white streaks from the moving headlamps.

"Sulfur," she answers. "It won't hurt to breathe it."

She doesn't know if her words are a lie or not, it's just a line she always uses. Yet it must be true. The scent has never harmed her.

She blinks rapidly and focuses. Five shapes are emerging within the blackness.

Asif and Jack are standing together. Adam is alone and Kerry is clinging to Max.

"You have hold of the wrong man," Alex tells her.

"Oh!" Kerry gasps loudly. "Oh! I'm so sorry!"

She grips Adam as if it is his fault while Max and he only laugh.

Her apologies are high-pitched and to Alex, annoying. The tone of her voice is grating on her nerves.

"This is so weird," Jack announces.

The six people are standing in what appears to be a sealed metallic eight-foot box. The box is an illusion. A trick of the eye.

"Is this the bunker?" Asif asks. He finds the nearest wall and raps on it. The noise sounds far louder than it really is. Metallic and cold.

"No. Follow me."

She squeezes through the group until one side of the wall becomes clearly illuminated.

A thin door.

It is barely visible and only seen by its smooth lines of separation. There is no handle, only rusty stains from where one used to be attached.

She presses firmly. The door rebounds a little, enough for her to jam her fingers around and widen the gap.

It opens halfway into a stone-lined hallway. The walls are rock and damp, sharp too, and with jagged pieces poking out.

The ground is fairly sturdy.

"In a line behind me please," she says and turns left. "Watch you don't rip your clothing."

The group follows with unsure baby steps. The temperature drop is immense and, as always, she shivers deeply.

"Watch your footing too," she warns.

The ground does appear flat, almost like concrete, yet sharp stone hazards erupt from the surface and if one person falls in the narrow walkway, they will likely all cascade down like dominoes. Thick tentacles of branches erupt from the rock, some are graced with tiny green buds on the end.

"How does this grow from rock!" Asif cries. He stops briefly to touch the small buds in wonder. "With no sunlight or water?"

"Nature, I guess," Alex says. "Nature does what it wants."

Twenty-two steps until they need to turn. The buds always catch the eye of someone. They look fresh and vibrant and don't belong under the earth.

"It's so cold," Kerry complains. The rest agree in mumbles. She isn't wrong. The rocks do feel like bitter chunks of ice. The air holds and perhaps craves a low temperature.

At step ten, Alex pauses.

"In a moment, we will enter a former storage room. This is where the bodies were found."

"Excuse me! What bodies!" Kerry gasps.

"It's on the website," she explains. "I detailed the official reports."

"Yes, I read it," Asif speaks up. He is at the back of the line and Alex knows he still has his mobile phone hidden on his person. She is no fool and only four were left inside her van. He must believe she cannot count.

"It was a fascinating read," he adds.

"What bodies!" Kerry cries again. "It is haunted down here!"

'Here, here, here.'

Her shrillness echoes.

"I don't believe in ghosts," Max announces. "But yeah, what bodies?"

There is always someone who hasn't read the website details properly. People, Alex notices, tend to become far too excited over a new place to explore, especially if visiting is a rare opportunity. Many people want to try urban, rural, or underground exploration, but the vast majority fear being caught or becoming trapped. A website such as hers makes people feel comforted by professionalism. They do not feel the need to bore themselves with the descriptions and details. They assume that if her website is online, then her tour is safe and perhaps even dull with an added illusion of danger. Most people skip through until they reach the testimonials and make the assumption the praise for her tour is genuine.

"Near the end of World War Two, a German aircraft was heading towards this village. Military officers, five men, and one woman rushed down into this bunker, and after the danger passed, they couldn't get back out. This place was so secret that not many people even knew about it. It was assumed they'd left the area without telling anyone. No one knew they were stuck. An underground survey was conducted years later, and the bunker was opened. Five men were still inside. Some say they'd resorted to cannibalism and suicide or went utterly insane. Whatever they found, the bunkers were sealed again."

"That's horrible," Asif says. "Seriously."

"Yes, it was. Now, follow me and watch your heads."

"Wait, what became of the woman? Do you mean they ate her?"

"No one knows."

The next room has a low opening and is very narrow and confining, little more than a cupboard. The walls still have empty metal shelving pushed up on each side and a single empty filing cabinet. They hold nothing but thick dust, filth, and old memories.

"Straight through here," Alex tells her group. "And then we take a sharp right. Hands and knees only, people. Crawl and don't crouch. It's a very low passage."

She pushes a small half hatch open and bends. They will have to shuffle along for a short amount of time. It can be awkward and she herself often has bruised elbows and knees from such activity.

It becomes colder almost immediately. She sees her breath turn to vapor. This is the part she hates the most. She is not claustrophobic. She only fears that someone might panic and stay behind, retrace their steps, and find they cannot get out. The hatch they entered is one-way only.

"Crawl behind me, it's safe," she says. "I'll help you up on the other side."

She makes her way through. The tight passage is not big enough to turn. She moves along quickly.

She wishes she could stop to enjoy the moment. The tunnel is like a symbol of rebirth, a metaphorical birth canal. The first time she crawled through, her own renewal was close to occurring.

They are in the underworld completely. A silent and mysteriously harrowing land. Often, she prefers the still environment to the surface world.

She feels her way steadily until she is out. She stands up and brushes herself down. She is in a small room carved out purely from rock. Wooden benches still line the sides where people were supposed to sit and wait for the danger of war to pass. A hallway once connected the rooms, but it collapsed some years ago.

Max is the first out. He bangs his head as he crawls and appears.

"Now I know why we need hard hats," he laughs.

Asif and Jack come next, followed by Kerry and Adam. All present and correct, she breathes a sigh of relief.

"This is the room," she tells them. "Where the men were found."

It isn't the truth, but it's close enough.

She gives each person a moment to think about how life might have ended for the forgotten people.

Not a difficult thing to accomplish in such wild, suffocating darkness.

"Now, this is where things get tricky. Follow me closely and use your hands to guide you. You may need to shuffle sideways. It's extremely tight in places."

She pushes at a narrow door. The scent of sulfur increases.

The rock wall facing her makes it appear as if the group is trapped. Shadows flicker, long and curious, sinister shadows. She can hear the steady trickle of water as she reaches out an arm.

There is plenty of space, although she can admit it doesn't look that way. She steps out and turns. She can walk forward in a straight line easily enough, but the biggest man, Max, will have to shuffle sideways, as will Kerry, whose shoulders are broad.

The group copies her movements. The rock walls are damp and stained red, it is becoming harder to breathe. Lower and lower they descend.

They need to walk ninety-one steps.

"I feel funny," she hears Kerry cry. "A bit dizzy. I can't breathe."

"It's fine. You're perfectly safe," Alex calls back. "This is a natural passage, and it's held for eons. There's plenty of air, too."

She can hear Adam mumbling softly, trying to calm her. Asif offers to push her and hold her hand.

Sometimes, she wonders if two tour guides would be better, one at the front and one at the back. This is the passage that causes difficulties the most. People who swear they are not fearful of tight places or darkness soon realize they actually are, and panic enjoys freezing bodies into place the most.

There is a way to go yet. They cannot become stuck and jammed. It just won't do.

"Not far," Alex shouts. "I promise. Through this gap is a huge chamber with plenty of space."

She feels a jolt behind her; it is Max. Even in the thick darkness, she can feel him smile and roll his eyes.

"Drama queen," he whispers.

Alex has the feeling he might like her. Still, she is not interested, even though he does seem like a good man. She only has one passion in life, and it is not other people.

"We're moving!" Adam yells.

"Well done, Kerry," the rest encourage her.

The girl is crying softly but shuffling. She really is braver and more determined than Alex guessed.

Step by step, they shuffle. Bodies close together. At step eighty, she stops and warns the group.

"The passage drops a little now. It's quite steep."

It is extremely slanted, it's almost like a slide. She locks her arms into place and walks the remaining eleven steps. It isn't enough to hold the group if one person tumbles, but it might slow a fast descent down.

Light glows softly in the distance. A warm amber glow, like a roaring fireplace, ready and waiting.

After the slope comes a very troubling part.

The bridge.

One more step. She comes to a stop and peers down.

Sometimes, for Alex, it feels as if she is standing on the very tip of the world, the edge of all that is unknown. It is one of her favorite places to stop and enjoy. The feeling of staring down into the wide chasm creates in her a sensation of utter insignificance.

Great wonders and enchantments exist under the earth. She knows this. Perhaps old magic was pushed down and out of sight by the building of homes, tarmac roads, and skyscrapers above. People forgot the old ways; the magic of nature, and it scurried away and hid.

"Stop behind me. Careful steps now," she calls. "Don't slip."

She throws out her arms as a weak and likely pointless barrier.

The group is clustered safely behind her. They all stand on the fairly wide ledge and crane their heads to look down.

"Why is it so misty?" Asif asks.

"I don't know," Alex tells him. "Vapor maybe."

"From where?"

She has no answer. The mist has always been present. It just is. Asif asks too many questions. Curiosity killed the cat.

"Where's the light coming from?" He asks.

"A battery-operated lamp. It helps a little. Look. The hardest bit," she points.

There is a narrow line to cross, a natural curved bridge made entirely of stone and dread. One false move and it's a never-ending fall into misty chaos and darkness.

Pretty vines wrap around the bridge like rope and give it a fairy tale feel.

"Oh shit no!" Kerry screams as she sees. "No, no, no. I'm not crossing that. No, I'm not!"

The bridge is just over a foot in width, there is no way back. They are far under the ground, further than they realize. Alex waits for the tantrum and protests of Kerry to stop echoing.

"It's the only way, the abandoned train station, the place you *all* came to see, is that way."

She points across the bridge.

For her, the rocky span is the equivalent of leaving one world and entering another. It is a new, forbidden realm. A world full of possibility. Beautifully fatal too, yet drenched in exhilaration and awe.

Kerry wobbles and falls onto her knees. She is taken by panic and sobs openly. Asif shuffles his way over and pats her on the back. He has become the official spokesperson for the others, the father or leader of the group.

"This is a bit... well, dangerous," he says. "Even for me and I once went into a shark cage."

"You did," Jack agrees brightly. "He really did. I've seen the photos," he proudly assures the others.

"Well, this isn't as scary as sharks, and it isn't slippery. Look, I'll show you," Alex tells them.

She focuses her light to check her footing and dances her way across the bridge with all the grace of an expert ballerina. Four steps, that's all it takes and no one from any group she's ever taken has fallen yet. Easy.

"Have you got any safety ropes?" Max asks. "This is awfully hazardous."

"No, because we don't need any. You can make it in two or three steps. Think of what you'll see when you cross."

"This is... not what I was expecting," Asif complains. "It's a health and safety nightmare."

"I agree," Jack says. "I think we should turn back."

"We can't," Alex tells him. "*This* is the way. You all knew the risks."

Asif rummages in his pockets and takes out what she thinks might be a coin. He throws it down into the chasm between them. The group holds their collective breath. No one hears the object land.

"Shit," he says. "That really is so deep."

They all claimed in their applications to want adventure and risk, yet when faced with such wishes and desires, they are each swarmed with fears and regrets.

How can crossing a thin and sturdy bridge feel more dangerous than a shark cage or climbing a treacherous mountain? Even Adam and his sailing hobby hold a larger hazard.

"Oh well," Max announces. "I suppose this is the thrill I wanted."

He takes a deep breath and walks steadily across the bridge without any issue at all. Alex understands that he is trying to impress her, and his subtle plan works.

"That's it!" She says, pleased. "That was perfect. The rest of you, aim for my light and you won't fall. You're overthinking it."

Asif steps forward and then back. He repeats the motion several times.

He behaves like a cat preparing to jump onto a high surface. A cat that doubts its own ability. Besides, human psychology comes into play. He does not want to be seen as weak. He will cross and Alex knows it.

Adam pushes his way forward.

"I'll do it. I want to see that train station."

He stands and blinks rapidly. Max holds out his hand and Alex grips Max by his jacket. A human chain that resembles paper cut-out figures.

Adam crosses easily. Jack follows with his arms out for balance like a theatrical tightrope walker. Only Kerry and Asif remain.

Come on, we're wasting time, Alex thinks.

Tick tock. She feels a wave of hunger and agitation, feelings that don't belong to her. They need to hurry. Time is growing short.

"Just cross!" She yells. "It's so easy!"

She listens to her anger and frustration echo and bounce. Behind her is a pitch-black tunnel, followed by a deep hole and a slight slope downwards, the last and easiest path of all. Delights lay beyond the pretty slope.

"Jack," Asif says. "Get ready to grab my hand."

His partner reaches out, now part of a longer human chain. Asif crosses in a half leap. Alex feels her throat constrict with terror. For a brief moment, she is sure he isn't going to make it. But yes, he has. He is in his partner's arms and laughing. Exhilarated and proud of himself, no doubt. Tiny pebbles scatter and fall down into the abyss.

Dramatic Kerry is last. She paces up and down the short ledge.

Now it's Adam who chooses to reach out. The rest support his weight. Kerry only has to step once, maybe twice, before she has hold of his hand.

"Come on Babe," he says. "Make us proud. One, two, three."

Kerry stops and does not move.

If she doesn't cross soon, I'll drag her over.

"Kerry, come on, it's so simple," Max tells her. "Come on, in one, two, three."

She still does not move.

Shit! Come on!

"What's that behind you?" Adam gasps and points.

Kerry squeals and crosses the bridge in two wide and frightened steps.

It is a cruel and twisted trick and yet it works a treat.

"Idiot!" She shouts at him. "That's a horrible thing to do!"

Adam only chuckles in reply. Alex isn't at all bothered by the prank, the girl is across, and that's really all that matters.

"Right, this way," she says.

They hold on to each other's clothing to maneuver down a thin but short dark tunnel.

A flat stretch of smooth stone ground faces them, the walls surrounding them create a natural rock dome. In the middle of the ground sits a perfectly round hole with interlaced vines surrounding it.

The hole looks absurdly dark. Almost as if someone painted a neat black circle with a soft brush and a patient hand.

Alex believes the hole looks quite like a cartoon somehow, a trickster drop.

Yet it is the place she first fell down and down, all that time ago. She only meant to peer down the hole long ago, but she fell, didn't she? She slipped and now look.

Shadows pass and create odd patterns as the group gathers around her.

"This is the drop. There is no ladder. You will fall into clear water, and it won't hurt a bit."

"Fucks sake!" Kerry gasps. "What kind of tour is this!"

Alex ignores her. She feels torn. Sometimes it's better for her to drop down first. The moment her tour groups hear the splash, they feel comforted. In this case, it might be better if she drops down last.

"Alex," Asif addresses her sternly. "It's not possible that a train station could ever be built this far down. I mean, come on! What's really going on here? I think we've all been patient and given you the benefit of the doubt enough."

It took the last group much less time to become suspicious.

She feels her blood run cold. She knew he was the one she had to watch the most.

Still, others have asked the very same question at some point.

"It might feel as though we're deep under the earth, but our path has been deceiving. An illusion. Besides, there is no actual direct route to get to it. So we had to go down and then up. It's disorientating, I agree. Besides, why would I bring you down here and lie?" She says.

"Maybe you're going to murder us?" Kerry suggests.

"Oh sure, five against one! That's great odds. Guys, I run a business. I can't afford to mess people around."

She knows she sounds convincing. She has had more time than most to perfect her act.

She picks up a loose stone and drops it down the hole. The splash that follows is loud enough for everyone to hear.

"Water see, but honestly, if you'd rather go back, then it's fine," Alex smiles and calls their bluff.

"I'm not going over that bridge again," Kerry says. "No fucking way."

"Then the only way is down and then up. Does anyone want to go first?"

Alex looks at Max. She only has enough light from the headlamps everyone wears, but it's enough to see his expression. Uncertainty, doubt.

"How long is the drop?" He asks.

"Five, maybe six foot. There's a large pool of water which will be cold, but it's pure too. It's deep enough to cushion the drop, but you can touch the bottom if you stretch."

"Right... I don't know. Sorry."

This from the man who shuffled his way through tight caves spelunking and climbed a huge mountain in the bitter cold?

"If I go first," Alex tells them. "It means you *will* have to follow me. You won't find your way back out without me."

"I remember the way," Asif announces with confidence.

"You might think you do, but you don't. If you become lost, I might never find you."

Adam crouches down and takes off his hard hat. He uses the light to peer down the hole. It is utterly black; light cannot penetrate such fearsome darkness.

"Fuck it, I'll go," he grins. "I'll do it."

Alex feels the warmth of relief flood her limbs. So far, this has been one of her worst tours. She wonders if she chose the wrong people, but of course, it's too late now.

Adam positions himself on the lip of the hole and drops his legs down. He pinches his nose and grins.

"See you in a moment!" And just like that, he is gone. They all hear a loud splash of impact.

Alex and the group wait and wait. Just as she begins to feel a ripple of panic surfacing, she hears him.

"Woah! That was easy!" He yells. "Really easy."

The mood lightens dramatically, tensed bodies loosen. Now the other four are smiling and cannot wait to drop down into what only seems to be oblivion. Max goes next, followed by a hesitant Jack. Asif still seems unsure until he hears the voice of his partner reassuring him. He drops down and half screams his way. Kerry is the last, as Alex expected she would be. Woman to woman, Kerry wants an answer to her suspicions.

"Is there really an abandoned train station?" she says.

"Yes."

"Look at me, look me in the eye, and say it."

Alex does. "Yes," she repeats. "There is."

"You're lying. I know it."

"I'm not," Alex laughs. "I swear. Now please, I'll follow you."

"You better," she hisses and narrows her eyes. "Adam, get ready to help me."

In the time it takes Alex to blink, the girl is gone. Down into chaos and eternal dark.

She waits a moment, just a brief slice of time to enjoy the silence and have a moment alone.

"Alex?" She hears. "ALEX!"

Do they each believe she has abandoned them? The thought makes her smile.

"ALEX?"

"Coming," she shouts and drops.

It is easy to lift themselves out of the pool using the ledges. It is more like a secret bathing area kept aside for ancient goddesses needing privacy to sing and bathe.

On one rock wall is a cave painting of a large and intricate tree, blessed with spiraling branches, a thick trunk, and curly roots. Stick bodies lay at the roots.

"Look at this," she tells her group. She shines her light onto the rock art. "Isn't it beautiful?"

"How old is it?" Jack asks. He is shivering wildly. They all are.

"Ancient, I suppose. Prehistoric art."

"Is it by those Netherlands people?" Kerry shrieks.

The group chuckles.

"Neanderthals is the word you want," Max corrects her.

"Well, maybe they came from the Netherlands," she snaps back.

Alex remains silent. The girl might be speaking the truth in part, and she doesn't even know it. Yet she can't be certain of that. How could anyone be sure?

She feels a wave of impatience that makes her jolt where she stands. They need to rush.

"Do people know about this art?" Asif asks. "Anthropologists, I mean?"

"I don't know. I guess so. Follow me," she insists. "And stay close."

The group heads through a narrow passageway, a natural parting of jagged stone. The passage leads to a pleasantly slanted slope. Water defies gravity and runs across. Each spiral of water creates pretty and intricate patterns on the rock. Large circular boulders stand on each side of them like guardians. Dark green moss grows in abundance. An amber glow is present, more battery-powered lights, yet it is now only slight. They stand inside a large chamber with a tall cathedral-style ceiling. Instead of expertly painted religious images above, long stalactites hang down with fierce points. The acoustics of the chamber are perfect. All Alex can hear is the gentle pitter-patter of water and boots scuffling against rocks. The sight is something beautiful to behold. An alien world and yet not.

"How deep are we?" Max appears by her side.

She shrugs. She doesn't know the answer.

"Just deep, I guess."

"Where's the station?" Asif says. "I'm finding it harder and harder to believe there's one down here."

"Just around this corner. I promise," she lies.

A huge boulder stands in front of her. The shape constantly re-minds her of a human face; it always has. There is a hollow part for a single eye, a jagged ridge for the nose, and an open gap for the mouth. Branches embrace the formation and curl in pretty patterns.

Asif must see the resemblance of a face, too. He cannot resist. He takes his phone out, shakes it free of water, and tries to snap a photograph.

"Sorry," he mumbles.

It doesn't matter, not now. No one will ever find the gadget and it probably won't work, anyway.

"Come on," she says. "What you see next will make it all worthwhile."

The group pushes their collective doubts aside and renews their faith in her once more. They blindly follow around the corner. In a single line, they walk behind her.

No one expects to see what it is they actually witness. How could anyone guess?

Tree roots.

Thick roots of impossible size and multitude are tangled in unfathomable gnarled knots that resemble plaited hair. Each distinct root is a meter across at least. Together, they create a huge mass of epic proportions, the size of a standard two-story house or bigger. The roots twist and wrap in a curiously beautiful pattern. A vibrant life force that moves and thuds like a heartbeat.

The sight is dark brown and black in color, with golden, shimmering sap dripping down in pretty spirals. The scent of the sap is sulfur.

Tiny buds sprinkle the tree, green in color and seemingly alive. They shudder and move very slightly.

The very top of the tree, far above the ground, spreads out and weaves off to create a lush and perfectly vibrant forest. The land belongs to it and likely always has. Perhaps the entire surface of Earth belongs to it also.

Alex often wonders if the clever Norse people witnessed the marvel somehow for themselves many years ago, and therefore, created the legends of the Yggdrasill, The World Tree. Or perhaps it is something else entirely. The heart and valves of the entire planet, mother nature, a true Gia, the vital organ.

She does not know. Ideas are not proof.

She has her own name for the tree that is alive and aware.

"What the hell is this?" Asif asks. She can hear the shock in his voice, but something else too, wonder and amazement. He is astonished. It happens to everyone, as it once happened to her.

"It's a god," Alex replies. "A goddess too, and everything else in between. Perhaps the oldest god of all."

Her words are her truth.

Darkness, hate, menace, power, corruption. Yet balance, harmony, love, and light.

A contradiction, a conflict formed into branches, roots, buds, leaves, sap, and bark.

Opposites in harmony. A tree of Yin and Yang principles.

She steps forward and climbs gently onto the lowest roots. The tendrils continue down and penetrate deep into the earth and might go on forever. She wipes a sliver of the sap away with her finger and licks the residue.

The substance is what keeps her alive, and she has been alive and young for many decades. A true fountain of youth, amber nectar, the Ambrosia of Greek mythology.

A deep rumbling begins. The sound comes from all directions, above and below, left and right.

"What's happening?" Kerry cries. "What the fuck is this?"

"Hunger," Alex answers her. "That's the sound of hunger."

***

She was one of the six to become locked under the earth in nineteen forty-five. The lone woman everyone assumes was gobbled up greedily by the five wicked men.

There had been rumors in the small village of an impending attack from the air.

The Germans, someone in charge claimed, knew about the secret base under the ground and knew of its exact location.

Maps were held inside the hidden rooms, along with confidential information that contained all manner of illicit knowledge on the enemy.

Her role was secretarial, yet as the brutal air-raid siren sounded, she fled, pulled along by another officer, all scampering away like wild rabbits into burrows.

It took two hours of waiting underground before they understood no bombs had fallen. Another hour before they realized they could not leave. The hidden hatch they worked hard to conceal so artfully failed to open. A snapped and badly made handle was all it took. A further ten hours passed, full of desperate shouts and screams no one above could hear.

There were no other military personnel in the village, only quiet families and people sick and tired of a war that never seemed to end.

No one came. Hour after hour passed.

Desperation increased. Wild panic took hold.

Deliberate neglect, forgotten, accidental miscommunication, or sabotage. None of the six knew what might have happened, but they each knew their fate, each knew they were damned.

Alone underground with five hungry, increasingly unhinged men, she faced a crisis of her own. She saw the way a couple of the men looked at her; she knew their plans and thoughts without words needing to be spoken. Only one man was willing to defend her.

As fierce arguments raged, as fighting erupted, she escaped the room and squeezed herself through tight passages and narrow gaps.

She decided she would rather die lost inside the belly of the earth than be killed at the hands of crazed, frightened men turned into savages.

Yet she did not die, instead, she found new life.

Wandering in blackness, without even her own sight for company, she heard her name being called. Felt the pull of something inhuman luring her, something new and strong and fierce. Something she herself aspired to be.

'Alexandra, Alexandra.'

A female voice, maternal, calling to her. She followed, half delirious with thirst and wretched with fear.

Through narrow passages she later came to widen, she crawled. Across a treacherous bridge seeking to destroy her, she sped. Until she fell down into a hole of bitterly cold water. Her ankle broke, her will to survive ceased. She stumbled blindly, torn inside by rich agony, certain the men were behind her, but no. She came across her salvation instead.

A dark god waited. A willful malevolent force. A friend of chaos and disharmony. There it stood as if it had always been, and perhaps it always had.

The source. The first seed.

Twisted branches stretched out and welcomed her, embraced her. Tiny saplings entered her mouth and bloodstream until they blossomed and grew inside her. She healed, mind, body, and spirit.

Alex changed. A rebirth under the ground. A companion for an ancient force, a symbiotic relationship of vast difference.

She lay in the coldest of embraces for hours, revived and complete.

A favor was asked of her, not spoken aloud but told to her by the sharp whispers of slithering branches.

Soon after, she reversed her journey, fetched the trapped men, and promised them all she had a way out.

Death was the only exit for four of them. No remorse was given, for they were willing to have none for her. The fifth was spared, the one who tried to defend her, Vince.

He joined her in worship.

***

She hears the click of a button, comes back to herself, and sees a bright flash of light. Asif with his phone camera again. He is thrilled.

"This is amazing!" He says and steps forward, pulling an open-mouthed Jack along with him. "Better than seeing those sharks. Better than any train station! I mean... What is this!"

The others follow him and walk closer. Only Kerry is afraid, but Adam pulls her forward.

Alex chooses to step back.

Over the years, the darkest of gods has grown immensely. The impossible tree was dormant when she found it, in a sleep state, a stasis. Forgotten and alone, cast aside and only in existence inside myth and legend. She began the process.

Waking fully takes decades.

Alex brings it food, and that is her role, her honor. She is a care-taker. She brings five people once a month without fail. In return, she does not age or suffer any illness. The sap is hers to take.

Time is not her enemy.

She was given an opportunity. She was gifted a chance to live, and she snatched it with greedy hands. A pact bound by branches and blood.

It is an opportunity not without penalties. Guilt swarms her. Knowledge of future events plagues her. The end is close.

Perhaps time will be her enemy after all.

The five, her group is entranced by the incredible sight before them, hypnotized by its strange and gloriously alluring beauty.

Truly, the sight does look magical, something only imagined in old fairy tale books or wild fantasy movies. It carries an energy of power, a thrum of strength.

In a line, they step closer, closer. Mesmerized. Utterly compelled.

Adam is the first to fall.

A vine, seemingly with a snake-like life of its own, scrapes across rock and stealthily wraps around his ankle. He does not hear or see its approach. With a swift jerk, he is knocked off his feet and is soon hanging in the air, caught in a deadly and simple trap. A thick vine strikes without mercy and forces its way down his throat. He flails wildly in his panic and chokes.

One down.

The attacks happen quickly. A shock and awe technique. Escape is impossible. Tendrils of vine and branch explode from the tree roots and constrict each person tightly.

Screams of horror and terror erupt from each mouth.

The tree roots part and swallow Asif whole. He barely has time to react or scream. Two down.

Jack lashes out in a wild frenzy. Deadly serpent roots arrive and wrap around his throat. He dies quickly, not by strangulation, Alex believes, but from a quickly broken neck. Three down.

Kerry is catatonic, a pitiful sight. She is the one who screamed the loudest and now is the quietest of them all. She sits on the hard floor, all comprehension lost, overwhelmed by shock. A vine encircles her like a rope. Her body is squeezed until an explosion occurs.

Warm blood sprays. Meat, bone, and brain tissue arrive in a shower. Four down.

It is always so messy, mealtime.

"WHY!" Max yells at her, a terrible echo follows.

She can hear the panic within the layers of his screams. She thought he might be the bravest, but no. Everyone, it seems, is just as scared as the other when confronted with unknown concepts and death.

He spins and tries to run. No hope. Survival is not an option.

Thick vines creep towards him with quick, slithering motions. One vine constricts his waist, the others reach eagerly for his legs.

Alex closes her eyes. He seems like a good person; she does not want to witness his ending.

A tear falls down her face, her heart hurts. Truly, she hates what she must do.

Max's screams switch to wails of scorching hot agony.

Soon there is nothing but bloody gurgles and silence. Five down. Gone. Eaten, absorbed. Over in mere seconds.

A single booted foot, torn away at the ankle, lands by her feet. A tentacle of vine scurries quickly and swipes it away as if afraid she might want it.

The blood, mess, and ruin will vanish soon. Every part will be used as nourishment by the roots. The roots will feed the forest above and the forest will grow wildly.

Alex walks over to the tree and embraces the bark and the firm roots. She cannot help but feel love. She has tried many times to fight the feeling but fails on each attempt. She is joined somehow, linked with invisible chains and adoration.

She wants to stay, just for a short time, with the one she worships and feeds. She has time.

Vince was right. Tour groups are easy.

The idea has turned out to be one of his best. Snatching people from the street was always so hard. In a new age of cameras and heavy monitoring, such activity became an impossibility.

At least now, the villagers above are safe. Not that she cares, but still, they will have a role to play when the time comes and it must come, no matter what she does to delay the inevitable. She knows that.

Her god is a dark-natured god, with twisted plans and wretchedness for a beating heart. Spite for flesh and vileness for leaves.

Her god is glorious and with vibrant plans and sap for blood.

All she can do is feed it and hold it back. It demands a tithe be paid in bone and souls. To deprive her god of nourishment is to invite destruction on all. And yet, it wants more. Much more.

Can it see the tarmac and steel laced lands from the eyes and memories of its victims, its food?

Does it feel the testing of terrible weapons on its surface, the drop of every bomb? The cutting of every tree, the ruin of the oceans? Can it taste the poison?

It must, for it wants to cleanse the world, and create anew. A flood of nature and not of water, a burning tide of blood and fury.

It wants to rise; it wants to reclaim its surface, its flesh.

Mother nature wants rid of her children.

✱✱✱

It is hours later, and she has found her way out easily. Three passageways, one short climb, one hidden ladder, and two flimsy doors are all it takes. She emerges close to the forest, on the border that is closer than it was.

Sunlight will soon be rising.

"You okay?" Vince asks. He is waiting for her as always.

The barman, the player of a double role. Her partner in many crimes.

"I'm fine," Alex tells him.

"Is it time?" He looks around the woodland as if sensing a deep change.

"Not yet," she says. "But very soon."

"What can we do?" He whispers.

She puts her fingers to her lips. He must be quiet. The trees themselves have ears and eyes. Besides, she has no idea. Darkness is rising, that she knows for sure. She can feel it. Forbidden knowledge coursing through her veins.

"Ten meters," Vince says. "Overnight, the forest grew ten meters. That's double what it grew last month."

She nods. How can she answer? There is nothing she can say. Perhaps the roots grew from a seed of divinity eons ago in a forgotten world from before, perhaps the strange god is mother nature herself. A true world tree.

Her god is the darkest of all lights. The origin of all that slithers and crawls, of all that grows. A destroyer.

Nemesis and hope entangled.

Humanity, she knows, does not sense the approach of such horrors.

Nature is preparing to fight, and she longs to devour the world. The lands of skyscrapers, metal, and iron will fall. And the people? She does not dare to imagine.

Still, she will hold such a force back for as long as she dares.

Rather five a month be sacrificed than all.

One Month Later

Alex walks into the small pub with great purpose. She is set to meet five carefully vetted individuals, chosen by herself. Many applied, people always do, and she remains selective in who she picks.

BEAUTIFUL THINGS WAIT IN THE NIGHT

Eve jerked in her sleep and woke herself. She blinked twice, startled, and pulled her old blankets far over her head.

Sorrow and anxiety began immediately, and without mercy. The light of morning, however warm, was always too cold for her.

No, she would not face another day of horror. She would stay in her bed and feign illness, or something, anything.

It seemed to her that having to get up was a vile act of cruelty and a thing she never agreed to. There were always those first few seconds of bliss upon waking, before the painful truth and reality of her existence hit her.

And who was she inside her dreams? She was wild and free, unchained and running with a pack of soft-haired wolves. She was a princess, a warrior, a mythical Greek goddess of divinity emerging from a pretty seashell.

She much preferred her sleeping world of dreams rather than the darkness she faced daily.

Waking up *always* came as a nasty shock, for as far back as she could recall. Frozen water thrown onto the flames of fantasy that occurred inside her mind. Dread swarmed her body as she heard a familiar mumbling voice approach. If only she could halt time, or slip through the back of an old wardrobe door and live a whole new life with magical lions and snow queens.

The hammering on her bedroom door began immediately.

"Get up," her mother yelled. "Tend to the children. I'm sick."

Not sick at all, but hungover or still drunk.

Resistance was pointless.

"Okay," she answered. "Two minutes."

Mother. Some people claimed the word itself was the most beautiful in all the English language. Two perfect syllables meant to invoke love and peace, nurturing and protection. For Eve, the word conjured pain and hate. She guessed the people who thought the word so beautiful had never known a mother like hers.

The woman did not deserve the title she gifted to herself, a name to call her without real meaning.

She threw back her few covers and forced herself up. There would be hell to pay if she didn't move quick enough.

Her feet hit the warm, bare wooden floorboards that changed to intolerable ice in winter.

She could already tell that the day would be bright and hot.

Heat cascaded through her too-thin curtains. A t-shirt and old jeans would do for her outfit, and that was all she had to wear, anyway. She dressed quickly, avoiding looking at herself in the single cracked mirror above her old dressing table.

She was tall and thin but thought of herself as odd and misshapen. Her limbs were long, all sharp angles and edges. Her thick dark hair fell down her back in waves. She longed to use the scissors and chop it all away.

Because she was fifteen, her mother had forbidden her.

She wiped her face wearily, feeling much older than her young years, and made her way down the twisted and treacherous stairs.

"Eve, Eve!" Her siblings cried.

Eve was the eldest of four and the only girl. Allister came next, aged twelve, then Max aged ten, and Alfie aged seven.

"Shhh, please," she begged. Eve hated sounds. Quick sudden noises and annoying repetitive sounds. They were her natural nemesis, a thing to cause her panic.

Her brothers tried hard to be quiet for her sake, but each child was a natural ball of loud, relentless energy.

She poured cereal into three chipped bowls, added the last of the milk, thankful it hadn't turned sour; and hustled the boys into the shabby living room so she couldn't hear them chewing.

She returned to the kitchen, hearing only blissful silence.

She checked the cupboards and rummaged for food as her own hunger pangs surfaced. Had she eaten the night before? No, she couldn't. There was only enough for her brothers.

There's hardly anything left. I hope Mum is planning on going shopping today. We don't even have any bread; she thought.

While it was on her mind, she walked back upstairs and knocked carefully on her mother's bedroom door. She waited for an answer and received nothing. She poked her head inside the rank-smelling room.

Empty vodka bottles littered the threadbare carpet, along with clothing and an overflowing ashtray. A pair of men's hairy feet hung out from underneath the faded duvet cover.

Another new man? One she found in the pub and will never see again, no doubt.

"Mum," she whispered. "We don't have any food left."

Her mother grumbled and lashed out.

"I've no money. Get the kids out of here. I'm sick I told you," she snapped.

Eve lingered, unsure of what to say.

"But…"

"I said get out, you stupid girl!"

Eve flinched and closed the door with a click, just as a shoe was launched in her direction.

Another average day in the house.

She had three weeks left of the six weeks' summer holidays, and her mother had been out drinking most evenings. A different man in her bed each night was becoming normal. Eve tried hard not to judge her. It wasn't her business; she supposed. But surely her own children should come first? At least, it looked that way for the other girls at school.

She always has money for vodka. Yet nothing for her own family. I'll ring Aunt Jean. She'll know what to do.

She jogged back downstairs and sent her brothers outside to play football. A game they each couldn't get enough of. In summer, they longed to play under the rays of the sun. In winter, they would scamper around the attic playing wild chase games until she felt afraid they would fall through the ceiling.

For a moment, she stood at the crooked back door, enjoying the view.

Her mother owned the house, inherited from Eve's Grandmother who had died inside the walls years before. She knew the home must have been a wonderful sight in its prime, although it was currently falling apart and drastically so.

After Eve was born, when she was three or maybe four, her mother won a lot of money. Enough to last her for her entire life if she was careful, but instead, she'd blown it all in months.

And like the children, the house was not loved or cared for. Neglect was rife.

Her mother also owned the large patch of barren land at the rear of the house. Vast woodland backed onto it, the woodland with the stone circle Eve spent most of her time wandering.

Their house was isolated, three miles away from the nearest small town, and built at the very bottom of a slope. Eve often thought the location made it look as if the house had been dropped by the hand of a giant and carelessly left behind. Forgotten, all alone.

She drank a glass of water and prayed the phone service hadn't been cut off again. Her spirits soared as she heard the distinctive tone. She dialed.

"Aunt Jean, it's Eve. I hate to ask but we have no food again and mum is sick," she said.

"Drunk, you mean?"

"Yes."

"Do you need me to come over?"

"Please, could you? I mean, it's the boys, their big appetite. Mum said we have no money again and..."

"Give me an hour," Jean sighed and put the phone down.

Eve sat down heavily.

Mum doesn't give me a choice, she reasoned. The children need to be fed. Maybe I can look for a job again? In the cafe in town after school? Then I can at least buy food.

At fifteen, Eve knew she had to stay in education. The small school they all attended and the one she hated. She had no friends of her own. She was mostly overlooked or avoided, but that was how she liked things to be. It felt safer to be ignored.

Deep down inside herself, Eve was growing intolerable of everything and everyone. She found humanity to be hypocritical, self-absorbed, and cruel. Yet how could she know differently or find the good when only darkness surrounded her? She could see no light and never had.

She knew other people might sense her aversion to them, and that's why she was overlooked. The walls she built around herself were strong ones, crafted purely from disappointment and turmoil.

Still, she felt she did not fit in, regardless. While the girls in her class spoke of having a marriage and children someday, the concept alone made her uncomfortable. She did not like boys, not in the way that was expected of her.

Sometimes she liked to believe she was a changeling. Swapped at birth by the good folk themselves.

Other times, she believed something crucial inside her was broken, smashed beyond repair. The stress and sounds of her home and school, the multitude of voices, were always too much, far too overwhelming. She liked to hide in layers of clothing, nestled away inside.

She longed for paper worlds created and written about in books. She longed for the peace of the woodlands and the quiet, calm, serenity of nature.

She considered anything other to be unbearable.

Eve knew she did not belong, and it broke her already crumbling heart.

She watched her siblings play football and sat quietly, thinking and waiting for her aunt, her mother's younger sister, to arrive. She heard a car pull up outside and ran to the cracked, distorted window to peek.

Jean climbed out of her small car and crossed to her boot, her face stern, ready for another raging argument, no doubt. She began unloading bags. Eve, beyond grateful, rushed out to help.

"Who owns that car?" Jean asked and pointed to the rusty land rover parked.

"Oh, I think it belongs to the man upstairs with Mum."

"Who is he?"

"I don't know. I only saw his foot."

Jean tutted loudly and cursed. The two carried several bags loaded with food inside.

"You're all like bloody orphans! Look at this mess! Does she do anything for you kids?"

"Not really. Well, she made mashed potato last week, the powdered kind," Eve answered. "I try to clean. It's just... well, pointless, I suppose. Everything is broken, and the sofa collapsed. The wood inside snapped. Some of the old paintings are gone too. I think she pawned them."

The loss of the paintings skillfully created by her grandfather devastated her. The images in oil were dusty and almost ruined, but still beautiful. One showed the standing stones in the woods that were so important to her, drenched in warm sunlight she could almost feel. Another was created of calm forest land with curious lights hanging like glitter above.

No doubt whoever brought them saw value in the frames and not the paintings themselves.

Jean leaned forward and brushed the hair from Eve's face. She flinched sharply and backed away.

"Sorry love. Go and wander your woods, get some fresh air and don't talk to strangers. I'm sorting this mess out and having a word with your mother. Tell the boys to stay outside."

Eve nodded. "Thank you, Aunt Jean," she said as she walked away. The pressure on her chest started to ease a little. The pain in her mind began to lift. Eve headed for the treeline, straight for her world.

"Stay outside," she called to her brothers as she sped up. "I'll be back soon."

She entered the woods. Her wild sanctuary. The one place on earth she felt safe.

The piece of existence that was something of her own.

She immediately felt overcome with deep relief, a sense of homecoming. The heavy tree canopy above her head offered her cool shade from the burning heat of the day. A flurry of birds erupted from a nearby tree and announced her arrival. She knew every tree well, every route. Every place to find pinecones and fresh berries. The woodland was hers. Her kingdom of nature. Her church of trees and grass.

She stopped briefly, for once, to enjoy sounds. The noise of the woodland revived her and not once did she ever feel anxiety in her surroundings. No judgment, and no scorn.

The woods never cared that her hair was unbrushed or her clothes old and torn. She was accepted, welcomed.

Twice, she paused to wrap her arms around thick, rough trees.

Eve favored two close spots in the vast woods. The ancient stone circle, The Dancers, and the large rugged, wild pond further away.

She headed for the circle first.

She hummed an old folk song her grandmother once taught her as she walked, effortlessly stepping over fallen branches and twigs.

Her grandmother also taught her local folklore, cures, and stories. Which foods in nature were good to eat and which might poison her. Which ones tasted good, and which were still edible but sour.

She recalled her stories of magical worlds as she walked. Tales of Fae Queens and beastly black dogs. The Prowlies, the Good Folk, and an old story of the stones themselves.

She said the special place was a marker or a doorway. An entrance to a different world. A portal. A place where time was not welcome and had no real meaning. The way into a land full of kindness and wonder. Yet it could also be a place of darkness and menace. Spite and hostility.

Local lore claimed the stones were rebellious witches caught dancing on the night of the full moon or cursed by a Christian God for sinning wildly on His most sacred day.

Eve adored the seven standing stones.

As a child, she believed women were still trapped inside the giant monoliths. She would knock on the moss-covered stones and offer to help free them and save them.

She would run into the woods to seek comfort and solace among the monoliths, only for her mother to scream loudly and drag her back out.

"It's a cursed place," she would shout. "Stay away!"

Eve did not believe in the curses of witches or of mighty and ancient gods.

As an almost adult, she believed the local lore originally came from the mouths of men purely to scare women, simply because those same men feared women might remember their roots to a powerful feminine Goddess or remember their desire to be free creatures, held down by no man.

From library books, she knew the old stones were astronomical in nature, a calendar of the heavens, a place to track the solar system, a way to observe the routes of the stars.

A sigh escaped Eve's lips as the collection of monoliths came into view. She always felt a pull towards them, an affinity as if they were a magnet.

For years, she had never seen another soul visit the fairly unknown standing stones, day or night. On that day, a girl roughly her own age lay sleeping on the one stone that had fallen years before.

She felt a wave of horror at the stranger's intrusion into her private world. She fought the powerful urge to run away.

This is my place. Should I leave? I can't stay now, can I?

The girl looked as if she was dreaming. Golden blonde hair spread around behind her while her bare feet hung from the stone. She wore a blue summer dress, the color of the clear sky above them.

With delicate steps, Eve turned, sorely disappointed. She would walk away and leave. There would be no more seeking solace within the circle if other people sought to do the same.

Instinct stopped her, a strange pull in her belly. She moved carefully and peered around a thick tree.

The girl was awake, sitting up, staring around her.

Has she seen me? Can she sense me? She's beautiful!

Eve wrapped her arms around her body as a chill rushed over her. The girl stood with the quick stealth of a cat and balanced delicately on the stone. She raised her arms and spun in a circle while she hummed a soft, half-familiar melody.

Eve couldn't take her eyes away from her. Heat rushed to her face as she gripped the rough tree bark.

She felt overwhelmed by the feeling of curiosity and deep shame for intruding on the girl's privacy. Still, she watched the stranger, hypnotized, compelled.

She thought she was glorious. The girl danced with abandon, a wild freedom she could only imagine. She felt reminded of the spinning ballerina figure in her old jewelry box, but the girl was not stuck or glued down. She was pure clarity.

"Come out, come out, wherever you are," the girl sang.

Abruptly, she stopped spinning and pointed straight towards the tree Eve hid behind.

Eve jolted and ran.

She raced through the woodland and fled straight to the pond.

Who was she! She was so perfect! But she saw me! She knew I was there! She'll think I'm such a freak, just like everyone else.

Throughout life, Eve walked with clumsy steps. Years before, when she tried to make friends, she always seemed to say or do the wrong things. People noticed, and they whispered cruel things. It was a familiar, predictable pattern, and it hurt.

To draw attention to herself in any way only invited pain and trouble.

And now, her own mother had a notorious reputation within the village, and people tarred her with the very same brush and expected her to be trouble, too.

No matter how quiet and unassuming she tried to be, people gave her a wide berth.

The apple doesn't fall far from the tree; they claimed. But yet it does. Sometimes it falls very far.

For hours, she lay on her back and gazed at the sky. She watched fluffy clouds drift lazily past and tried to ignore her inner turmoil.

She looked my age; I think? She might come to my school? She wouldn't want to be my friend. Maybe she belongs to the family in the village? The new people that moved into the big house on the hill?

She took off her old, torn trainers and lowered her feet into the pond. The chill cooled her down.

I wish I could be so free. Imagine being so beautiful and wild? So confident. Oh, how that must feel.

Tears poured down her face. Yet she couldn't understand why she was crying. She only felt she had witnessed something beautiful and now nothing in life would ever compare to those precious few seconds.

With great reluctance and a heavy heart, Eve walked home. It was getting late, and her brothers would be hungry. The girl filled her thoughts.

The evening passed slowly. Eve cooked while her mother stared at her with vicious eyes, the kind of eyes that peered into everyone else's business. The previous evening's make-up still stained her face in uneven blotches. Her lines and wrinkles stood out more prominently than usual. The sharp sneer on her features and the evil glimmer in her eyes meant trouble.

Eve tensed and waited for the inevitable storm to begin.

It was not a long wait.

"Always running to Jean, aren't you," she spat. "You couldn't wait to tell on me."

Eve ignored her. Her mother was a simmering pot as a constant state, forever ready to boil over.

"I just want to have fun. What's so wrong with that?" She continued.

Eve closed her eyes and stirred the casserole in the saucepan, grateful her aunt had gifted them all fresh vegetables to eat. Outside the kitchen window, her siblings ran around in a game of chase, content in each other's company and happy to use up the last of the sunshine.

Just say it! Tell her what you think. Keep trying. She needs to be responsible. She needs to wake up.

"You're a mother. Just look at the boys and me. You have four children. You spend money on vodka instead of food for us all. You make life tough for me. You're always drunk too. I..."

Her mother scraped her chair back abruptly. She crossed the kitchen in two thunderous strides and slapped her hard across the face.

"Always violence, that's always your answer!" Eve cried.

She felt no shock, no surprise. Her body was already scarred and bruised from her mother's drunken rages and attacks.

"Stay out of my business!" Her mother screamed. "I wish I never had you."

The same old, overused line she always yelled. At least once a week, she had to hear those same terrible words strike her.

"Fine, look after your own kids!"

Eve turned and ran upstairs. On the landing, a greasy-looking man came out of the bathroom. She gasped in alarm.

"Hello pretty," he leered. "Why the rush?"

He made a grab for her as she ducked.

She ran into her bedroom, slammed the door, and wedged an old chair underneath the handle. She crawled under her lopsided dressing table and curled herself into a ball.

I hate my life; I hate it. I hate myself; I hate this place. I hate everything.

Nobody thought to check on her. All evening, the sounds of giggles and drunken laughter from downstairs reached her. She clamped her hands over her ears in protest and whined.

Is this what life is? Pain and stress? Is this it?

Her reality, the world she knew, was not for her.

She wondered if she should end it all and escape. Downstairs, in a small drawer, there were boxes of pills that belonged to her mother.

She longed to swallow them and fall asleep forever. Lost in a permanent dream.

But what about my brothers?

Life would become too hard for them. One, likely the eldest, would surely become her mother's target instead of her.

Her siblings were her tie to the world, the anchor that kept her alive.

By ten at night, she listened as her brothers were hustled to bed, crying from sheer tiredness. By eleven, Eve couldn't stand the man's booming and drunken laughter anymore. She opened her window as wide as she could get it and climbed out.

She hung from the windowsill, more graceful than she imagined herself to be, and dropped roughly onto the grass. It was a technique she had perfected over the years.

She raced through the night to the only place she felt safe. Her standing stones with darkness as her cover to hide.

149

The moon shone brightly and gave her enough light to guide her way. She broke the treeline, the transition point from the world she hated into the one she adored, and instantly felt calmer. The woodland greeted her with a chilly embrace.

Eve ran straight for her seven stones and almost collapsed with joy to find herself alone.

For a few moments, she sat by her favorite monolith and wrapped her arms around the moss-covered coolness.

A sense of returning home rushed over her. The heavy silence of the night gifted her all the comfort she needed.

I wish I could just stay here. Or sink into the ground and disappear.

For her, every moment of life seemed to mean trauma. The bad outweighed the good. The cruelty outweighed any scrap of compassion. She only knew pain and the bitter emptiness that left the biggest of all chasms inside. Where was the beauty people spoke of? The love and glory of life?

She wrapped her arms around herself and listened to the sounds of the night. An owl as it hunted far away. A rabbit scuttling through the woods, a heavier noise, likely a pretty and nimble-footed fox.

Her sensitive hearing picked up a new sound. One she hadn't heard in the woodland before and one that didn't belong. The gentle melody of a flute. The tones were complex and low. She could almost feel the vibration.

She scrambled up and gazed around her.

No one. So where is it coming from?

The sound became louder, closer. The tones made Eve flinch as she spun wildly in confusion.

The melody of the song felt familiar to her. A half-forgotten memory buried somewhere deep inside.

Wasn't it a lullaby? Hadn't she heard the song when she was a child? Was it the one her father once sang to her before he left and ran?

Her friendly woodland forest, the one place that had always welcomed her, became coldly indifferent. In the vast darkness, the night seemed to curl in on itself until the pitch blackness of the woods pressed down and down.

A rush of heat swept past her, a breeze emanating from a place unseen. The flute sounds grew louder. Eve clapped her hands over her ears as her mind rippled in pain. Electricity shimmered in the night air. Her ears popped. Dizziness took hold until she crumpled to the chilly ground.

Sounds of light laughter followed, the curious feeling of being jostled among a crowd, sunshine, and warmth. Still, she sat alone, hidden within the stones.

Two worlds collided. Two layers met.

A light shone above the tree canopy, brighter and bigger than the moon. Cool blue in color, vibrant and immense.

Eve felt a pull in her belly. A yank from invisible hands. She squeezed her eyes shut tightly and screamed. An eternity seemed to pass in frantic seconds. She felt the sensation of falling down, down, down into a void of nothingness.

Light came next, soft yellow, soothing light.

The sun. Is it morning? Did I fall asleep?

Not the sun. The beautiful blonde girl, with a glow of energy around her like the halo of an angel.

She crouched down and held Eve's chilly arms softly. Carefully, she wiped her lank hair from her face and smiled.

"Welcome, Eve," she said. "Tick-tock, it's time."

This can't be real!

Eve's eyes rolled back in her head as she fainted.

***

The moss felt damp beneath her body. Cold and, for once, unwelcoming. Warily, Eve opened her eyes.

The woods! What happened? Gosh, what a dream! I feel so sick.

She tried to stand on legs that could barely hold her. She used the stones to support her weight as she climbed to her feet.

Many times in her life, she had woken by the stones, curled up next to her safest of places. She wiped her face and fought off a wave of nausea. Without warning, she turned her head to the side and vomited.

She held her sore stomach and limped slowly home. She told herself she'd suffered a nightmare beside her stones, and nothing more.

Nobody greeted her as she used the broken front door. No one had noticed her absence or thought of her. The single clock told her it was only five in the morning.

Eve climbed the stairs and collapsed onto her bed.

She woke up for the second time in one day. Her stomach ached with hunger and emptiness. The hollow feeling was almost painful. She could not recall the last time she had eaten.

Downstairs, sounds resembling a riot met her ears.

Her mother was screaming at someone. Her brothers were crying. Doors slammed and a car started.

Is it Aunt Jean? Is she here?

Carefully, Eve sneaked a look from her bedroom window. The man, her mother's new friend, reversed in his land rover and drove away at high speed. *Another one running for the hills. Another one she drove away, just like my father.*

Her door handle rattled soon after. The wedged chair underneath stopped the enemy invasion.

"Get up you. Look after your brothers. I'm going to bed!"

"Okay," Eve muttered. "Please, be quiet."

More slamming doors. More crying sounds. Eve sat on the edge of her bed and cried. Her head pounded, her limbs felt weak and useless.

Was everything a dream? The girl and the flute? It must have been. I can't remember. Why can't I remember?

"Eve! Eve!" Her brothers yelled. In the room next door, her mother swore and smashed belongings.

She stood and left the room, down the stairs, and into the kitchen. No time to think or unravel her thoughts.

"What happened," she asked her oldest brother Allister.

"They argued. Mum tried to hit him. Can you make us some food?"

"Yes, but go outside. Give me a moment. Please."

She led her siblings out of the door.

Just make the food, shower, and then go to the stones.

Eve made toast and eggs. She took her own serving upstairs and ate it slowly. Within minutes, she started to feel better. She had a cold shower, the heating mechanism long since broken, changed her clothes, and left.

Back into the woods. Back into the vast woodland to think and to be alone.

She sat on her favorite stone and thought deeply. She came to the firm conclusion that she must have fallen asleep and had a strange dream, brought on by hunger and stress, no doubt. After all, what else could have happened?

It was just a dream. That's all. I dreamed of the girl because she was so very beautiful. I wanted to be her. No, I like her.

Her thoughts felt muddied and heavy. She only knew that the girl was perfect, in body and in soul.

For a brief moment, she closed her eyes. The sunlight seeped through the tree canopy and gave her warmth. The moss underneath her gave her comfort. Nature revived her.

I should pick some mushrooms and cook them for supper. That way we can save the food we have and…

"Hello, sleepyhead," sang a voice.

Eve snapped her eyes open and found herself gazing into two clear blue ones.

It's her!

"Oh," she gasped.

The girl had managed to sneak up on her. She jumped up and sat cross-legged on one of the stones. This time, she was dressed in a red embroidered skirt and a loose plain blouse. Her hair was wild and free and framed her face like a wild dandelion flower.

"Eve, the daydreamer," she grinned. "Daydreamers find me without ever needing to look."

"Sorry what? And how do you know my name? Who are you?"

"Silly Eve. I'm Celeste."

"Oh."

"You're a beacon," Celeste told her.

"I'm a what?"

Immediately, Eve believed the word must be an insult.

"A pretty beacon, but one with the wrong kind of glow."

This is so strange! What should I do? Is she unwell in her mind?

"I'm sorry. I don't know what you mean," Eve said. "Sorry, I should go."

"Apologizing for existing?"

"I… Sorry."

Celeste jumped down from the stone in one easy, quick motion and knelt down in front of her. Eve jolted in surprise. The hairs on her arms raised as heat flooded her face.

"Do you never wonder?" Celeste asked. "Seven stones, seven sins, seven days, seven seals, seven paths, seven virtues, seven sorrows."

"Umm…"

She must be sick. If she's part of the new family, I should take her home.

Eve blinked rapidly while her mind mapped out a quick route to the big house on the hill.

"Shall I take you home?" She asked. "I know the way."

"Silly Eve. It is me who came to take *you* home and no, you do not."

"What?"

The strange girl reached forward and placed her cool hands on Eve's face.

"See, seven stones, seven paths," she whispered. "Look, see. Peek. No eyes required."

Eve did not flinch at her touch; she did not feel afraid. Instead, she found herself welcoming the contact, needing it, a deep craving for more.

"I don't..."

She felt a sudden lurch inside herself, a quick sharp white-hot pain. A gut-wrenching plummet down followed. Anchor chains broke, the world blurred and shimmered until it fell away entirely. Eve found herself flying, up, up, up. Her body fell to the grass, a discarded rag doll. Her mind untethered and sped elsewhere. The sensation felt exhilarating and utterly impossible.

"Seven paths, seven futures," she heard Celeste say. "Emotions created the universe."

Fear began to spread. The woodland below her melted away. Darkness appeared in its place; blackness so thick she felt suffocated. A light appeared in the distance, a pale white light she felt drawn to. Without meaning to, the essence that was her raced towards it. Bright white light engulfed her, momentarily blinding.

She could not think or speak, she could only see. The harsh light faded.

A different scene appeared and wrapped around her. One full of despair so real she felt she could touch it.

She became an invisible witness to her own terrible demise.

She watched a future event in scenes without sound. She saw her own mother push her, caught in one of her fierce and drunken rages while snow lay piled high outside. One shove too many. A brutal blow. She saw herself fall down the stairs, over and over, until she landed in a tangle of twisted limbs. Her mother's face turned from anger to horror. Eve, herself lying dead on the floor. Blood pooled around her head, eyes wide and empty. Gone. Killed.

"That is path one," Celeste whispered. The voice of the girl seemed to ricochet all around her, an echo without source.

Eve had no limbs to move, none to run. No mouth to scream. Yet still, she was pulled away. To a second scene.

Herself among her stones. A little older. A pale figure, eyes wide and unblinking. A single bloody razor blade beside her, veins open. Life drained away. Given up, given in, and chosen to die in the one place she felt life.

"Path two." The gentle voice of Celeste rang out.

Another image bombarded her. Herself again, only much older. Alone in her mother's rotting house. Shivering in the cold. No job, no money for heat, and none for food. Alone and forgotten. Sadness and despair inside herself. Intolerable of everyone and everything. Lonely, so very alone, and with shards of agony piercing her solitary existence.

"Path three."

Eve again, but a vibrant, colorful scene. Laughing. Glowing with vibrancy and health. Hair shiny and thick, the widest of smiles on her face. Dressed in clean clothes, no jutting bones. No desperation, no loneliness, and playing with her brothers. Enjoying her life. Wild and free. Hope filled her.

"Path four."

The scene Eve yearned to keep watching faded away. Instead, she saw herself in a sterile hospital, a gray and old version of herself. Dying, surrounded by machinery. No family present. No loved ones. No one to miss her. Overlooked and neglected. A life spent wallowing in her own misery, unable to find or admit to her true self.

"That is path five."

Next, she saw herself huddled in a darkened doorway, a single blanket wrapped around her frail body. Grubby faced with pitiful eyes. Hollow cheeks, full of despair and pain. A piece of cardboard at her feet, coins collected, thrown at her.

"Path six."

Finally, the last vision. A funeral. Her own funeral. No one was in attendance. Her body in a simple box sent into flames without remorse or emotion. Even her brothers were absent. Eve, forgotten and abandoned by everyone. A life spent pushing people far away.

"Path seven."

Eve's vision turned black. The understanding of flying through space and time. A sensation of falling, lower and lower. Faster, then slowly, slowly. Back in her scarred body, the one she found so repulsive. Anchor in place. Chained back in position. Eyes open. Aware.

She vomited. Her body felt too heavy, weighed down impossibly. Fat tears fell as she struggled to understand, to comprehend the visions. Her mind spun furiously.

She couldn't breathe, her heart felt ruptured.

It couldn't be real. Such a view of all paths couldn't be true, could it? What was the purpose of showing her such misery? All but one scene was wretched and vile. Futures no one wanted.

Eve had always hoped she might escape the village, escape her house and flee. To know and understand that she never would, tore her soul into callous shreds.

She lay on the ground and curled herself into a ball, crying loudly.

"Shhh, shhh," Celeste soothed. "It's always hard the first time. There's a way to change things, Eve. There is a way."

The voice of the strange girl was full of pity, something else too. Solidarity and hope.

"What are you?" Eve croaked. Her body shook with brutal force. "How did you do that to me?"

"Seven paths. Seven, now you know," Celeste answered.

"Why? It's all so bad. Why?"

"Not all are bad."

Eve's own mind shuddered and struggled to fire.

This can't be happening! She's a Fae, One of the Good folk, she has to be!

"How do I get the good future? Please," Eve begged. It seemed urgent that she knew, vital. A matter of pure survival.

"You pay," Celeste told her. "You have to pay."

"But I don't have any money, I don't have anything. I…"

She began to panic; the future scenes came with rich feelings attached. Misery, the deepest hell she'd ever known. She craved the good future, yearned to feel that particular happiness that was so unknown to her.

"Please," Eve cried. "Tell me how."

Celeste leaned forward and whispered instructions. Secrets, plans, and guides.

Eve's whole body rippled in fear and understanding. The otherworldly girl stood and walked away calmly.

"Sun's end," she called as she left.

Eve could only sit in absolute shock.

I can't. I mustn't. I shouldn't. I can't. No… Can I?

She sat for hours.

Her inner turmoil felt different than usual. There was more at stake than herself.

Back and forth, her mind spiraled and raced in frantic circles. She asked herself questions, ones she could never know the answer to. The future scenes she had been forced to watch played and repeated in her mind. Was it a curse or a gift, to know, to experience and feel, to understand?

Thoughts tumbled over one another as she sought her answer.

I want a happy future so much. I have to pay.

Eve believed the girl was one of the Good folk, the Prowlies, the Fae her grandmother told her about, the beautiful shining ones from another, secret realm.

She saw the girl as special and kind, and she believed she must be helping her.

Do I want to be alone and forgotten, or killed by my mother? No. Do I have the right to do this? No. And if I don't do it? Knowing my future means I could change it, doesn't it?

No. She knew her mother well, knew rot was present inside her and always had been. She did not doubt the visions she saw. Her mother would murder her and likely claim Eve had slipped.

A tremor of anger rushed through her. Slowly, she climbed to her feet. It was time to claim her bright future.

What had she ever done to deserve such wretched futures? Nothing.

I want to see my brothers.

More than anything, she wanted to look into their eyes, a thing she so rarely did. She wanted to hold them, something she never did. She yearned to tell them she loved them, beautiful words she had never once spoken aloud.

She ran through her woods. Graceful and lithe until she broke the treeline. Her eyes landed on her siblings. She sprinted to the eldest and embraced him.

"Yuk! Get off!" He cried but laughed all the same.

She hugged the boys and tickled them, kicking their deflated football across the garden. Each boy raced for it.

She ran into the house, up the stairs, into her mother's bedroom.

Do this for them. For the boys. No, that's a lie. I'm doing this for myself.

At the sight of her mother, she faltered. All that hate contained within one person.

The way she behaved was often a power play. She enjoyed watching her own daughter suffer, and enjoyed watching anyone suffer. The pain inside others delighted her.

She's mean, she's nasty, bad inside. They'll take her somewhere else, a beautiful place where she can't hurt anyone.

"Get up mum," Eve said as she shook her. "I need you to come with me. There's something I have to show you."

"Go away!"

"You'll want to see this. It will change everything."

"Get out of here, NOW! I'm warning you."

"Please," Eve begged. "It's so important. You won't believe what I found!"

Eve's mother poked one eye out from underneath the duvet, curious.

"What is it?" She asked, her interest piqued.

"I can't explain. I have to show you."

Legs swung, movement. Eve's stomach plummeted while her heart soared in triumph. Inner conflict began its fight.

Outside, the sky began to darken as it announced its intention of becoming night. The sun began its descent. Time was growing short.

Tick-tock.

"I don't feel well," Eve's mother gasped. "I'm dizzy."

"You'll feel great when you see what I found. I never ask anything of you. Please come with me."

She handed her mother her scattered clothes picked up off the floor. She dressed slowly, only stopping for mouthfuls of vodka.

Eve's skin hissed and tingled as she watched, and tried to hurry her. Anxiety bubbled away in her stomach, a replacement for hunger.

"You're in deep trouble if this is a joke."

She ignored her mother's bitter words and insults as they walked down the stairs and out. Out into the garden, into the fading light.

"What am I supposed to see, then?"

"It's in the woods."

"I'm not going in there. Forget it. I'm going back to bed."

"No, please!"

Eve could feel her mother's resistance, her pull away, her desire to be in bed drunk overcame any curiosity.

Think quick! What can I say? Money!

"It's not far. It'll make us rich, I swear it. It's money."

Eve's mother turned and sneered. A vicious expression, full of hate and revulsion. Her vile eyes narrowed while a smile played on her lips.

"You better not be playing," she warned.

"I'm not, come on. You'll be rich. So very rich."

Eve called to her brothers to go inside and wait. They each agreed but carried on playing, eager to burn more energy.

Mother and daughter broke the treeline. This time, Eve felt different. She sensed eyes watching, peering at her, assessing and waiting. She felt sure she could hear whispers and secrets being swapped.

Her mother cursed and tripped.

"How much further? I'm not going near those damn stones," she snapped just as they came into view, each one silently waiting. Ancient and otherworldly.

They are a doorway! They were always a doorway. An entrance to another world.

In the distance, she heard the sound of a flute playing, low in tone and coming closer and closer.

I can still back out, can't I? I can change my mind.

She turned to her mother. The woman stood with her vodka bottle clutched tightly in her hand, swaying.

Remember when she locked me in the attic for days, remember when she told me she hated me and wished I was dead. Remember the kicks, the slaps, the abuse. Refusing to feed me. Hitting my brothers, leaving us alone night after night, hungry and scared. She's going to hurt me. She's never been nice. Not one part of her is good. When it snows, she'll murder me. In winter, I'll be dead.

Eve reminded herself of the past and her future paths. Deep within, she uncovered the fuel she needed, the bravery she yearned for. Yes, she could admit it. She wanted her mother gone.

"It's in the middle of the stones. A big bag of money. Go and look."

Her voice trembled with emotion, yet there was no regret, only hope.

Her mother carelessly discarded her empty bottle among the woodland and stepped forward.

Eve sensed a quick change in the air, a sensation of pressure and power.

She chose to step back.

The light began to shift rapidly. The surrounding woodland blurred and became unfocused. The last sounds of birdsong abruptly stopped. The ground itself vibrated slightly, pulsed, and warped as if moving position. Eve closed her eyes. A doorway opened; she could feel it. The air separated and folded.

I'm sorry, she thought as she closed her eyes, although she did not feel very sorry at all.

A strange feeling of finality took hold of her, judgment and revenge. Eve felt she was part of something far beyond her own small self, a cog in a wheel of vast impossibility.

The flute music ceased. A single scream sounded. Eve's eyes flew open. The scene in front of her appeared out of focus. It shimmered and flickered wildly, like a damaged movie reel.

A woman, a tall, wild, and fierce older woman with an animal skull for a crown stood in the middle of the stones. She wore shredded rags, and her dark hair was matted, thick, and filthy. Eve sank to the floor as the woman's narrowed yellow eyes met her own. One of her hands held a pitch-black lethal-looking dagger, the other hand gripped her terrified mother by a chunk full of hair.

"Pitiful," the wild woman spat. "Pitiful mortal, all black inside. I know her. Do you give her?" The woman addressed only Eve.

Her mother did not scream, could not. Her legs went out from underneath her as her body quaked in shock.

"Please," Eve tried to say. "I…"

This wasn't supposed to happen! Not this. Never this. They were meant to take her! What is she going to do?

She felt overwhelmed with the feeling that everything was wrong, that she had been tricked and deceived. A hand gripped her own, a small soft delicate hand. Eve looked up to see the girl, Celeste.

Celeste wiped a tear from her face and licked her own finger.

"Eve," she whispered. "It's a swap. Tell her yes. She swaps."

"But…"

"Tell her yes."

"Who is she?"

"She's my mother. Fiercer than yours and in a different way."

"What do I do?" Eve sobbed. She dared not speak the words she wanted so badly to say.

Celeste clutched her hand tightly.

Warmth spread across her limbs, borrowed or given by the strange magical girl. Within the layers of heat sat courage, bravery.

They're going to take her to a good place, that's all.

"Yes," Eve spoke up. "I give her."

In a single brutal movement, the wild woman gasped and reared back.

Eve's mother thrashed and jerked as dark blue energy flowed out from her body.

The light poured straight into the woman's mouth. A transference of energy, an eater of souls or devourer of essence.

The black knife sliced quickly across her mother's throat. Blood immediately poured in a heavy flow.

She fell face down, life gone. Steam began to rise from her fallen form. Smoke followed.

"Done," the wild woman hissed.

She raised her arms to the sky and wailed with power. Eve cringed at the booming noise and covered her ears with her hands. The sound vibrated deep within her bones. Vomit rose in her mouth. She swallowed the burn down painfully. Arms wrapped around her, Celeste held her and brought comfort.

"You killed her! What are you all?" Eve gasped. "Good folk?"

"We are something entirely different. See. A trade, a deal, a swap. The given provide more than the snatched."

Eve jolted as the girl placed her hands on her temples. Illusions fell, disguises faltered. Beautiful faces cracked apart like broken porcelain dolls. Monstrous images appeared in their place. Twisted faces full of rage and longing. Piercing lights, balls of energy. Forces, powers, both ancient and unrivaled.

Primal beings with a thousand aspects, names, and masks. Myth, legend, rumors, the origin of everything supernatural and unknown. Entities that were many and yet one, the first of everything.

Celeste leaned forward; she kissed Eve gently on her lips. Heat filled her, a connection made that could never be severed. Pure love transferred in a second. She smiled and vanished.

"NO!" Eve screamed. The pain of losing her felt a much sharper agony than the death of her own mother.

The wild woman bellowed like thunder and began to shake madly.

Her powerful image melted away as if she were made of nothing but candle wax. In her place stood a raven-haired young woman dressed in a glorious gown, beautiful and fierce. Vibrant with life.

The women switched to a gray misty form, swirling with energy, both stolen and taken.

The form twisted and writhed. Blue static hissed and flashed like lightning inside of it. It spun slowly. Eve saw images inside, faces of those lost, stolen, given away. The gray form spun and changed into a ball of crackling white light. She glimpsed tiny pinpricks glows inside before the light blinked out of existence.

"What are you?" She screamed.

A deep laugh ricocheted around the woodland. Eve scampered to her feet and ran.

***

Life had changed dramatically.

Search and rescue had been summoned by Jean to look for her lost mother, or look for a body. No trace of her was found, alive or dead. Specially trained dogs failed to pick up any scent or tracks. Each dog paused at the stones and refused to move further. Rumor spread that she had simply run away. The people of the village were not surprised. They only claimed they expected her to leave sooner than she did.

Eve herself claimed she lost sight of her.

Her mother wasn't the first to go missing in the forest, many had been lost before her. She became a number, one of many vanished.

Aunt Jean came to stay with the children and talked about making the move permanent. The house was cleaned and scrubbed. Repairs were organized.

Wholesome foods were cooked. The boys cried, of course. The smallest longed for his mother, while the older two felt silent relief they each dared not speak of.

Eve refused to leave her bedroom. By day three, she still refused to eat. Guilt poisoned her. Heartbreak too. She believed she deserved to die for what she'd done.

"Come for a walk in the woods with me," Jean ordered one bright afternoon.

"No," Eve replied. "I'm never going into those woods again."

"I need to show you something. Come on. I'm not taking no for an answer and it's time we had a serious talk. This family has a closet filled with skeletons that need air. Now, come on."

A curious feeling swept over Eve, deja-vu. Her mind reverted back to her own self days before, pleading with her mother to leave the house.

Jean pulled her blanket off and reached out.

"Please. For me," she said.

Reluctantly, Eve nodded and followed.

Maybe she's taking me off to face my own damnation. Maybe I'll have to join Mother and be killed. I deserve it, after all.

Eve followed Jean blindly. At the treeline, she hesitated, cold and afraid. She wrapped her arms around herself as if she expected to fall apart.

"Did I ever tell you about your father? No, I suppose I haven't. Your mother wouldn't allow it," Jean said as she pulled on Eve's hand to distract her. "Not the boy's father, your father, I mean."

The two walked forward slowly.

"No," Eve mumbled back. "He left me with mum and never came back. He didn't love me, I suppose."

Eve kicked at the ground, soft moss and fallen twigs. The ground she used to love and cherish was not her friend anymore.

"Let me tell you a story while we walk. Me and your mum, we weren't close as kids, you know that. She was a mean girl. Mean in her bones, right from the start, and then she met your father. Now, I'm not saying it was his fault or hers, but she... Well, she grew meaner, and then she had you. Your father wanted to take you away and leave her. All that terrible violence and drinking she started to do. Who could blame him? She wouldn't allow it. Then he vanished. He's left me, she said, and then, of course, she won all that money and wasted it."

"He ran away," Eve answered.

"Did he now? Are you certain? I know this land very well Eve, I grew up here just like you. When I was a girl, there were six standing stones in a circle, I swear it. Your father left and then there were seven."

"That can't be right," Eve interrupted.

"Well, it is, and I think it's high time you told me why there are now eight standing stones."

Eve jerked and stopped, her system flooded with brutal ice-cold. Her legs shook until her whole body shivered. She blinked rapidly, unsure of her own eyes and mind. She gazed ahead in wonder and terror.

Eight stones stood silently. Not seven, like always. Eight.

Each one stood old and moss-covered, as if they'd each been there a thousand or more years.

Eve fell to her knees as her head pounded.

"Aunt Jean," she gasped. "This is impossible."

How can this be? How?

Jean sighed and shook her head. "I think it's best you tell me everything," she said.

Eve did.

More days passed. Eve returned to her bedroom. She spent long periods staring at the wall in silence.

Jean persuaded her, little by little, to venture back out into the world.

"Just an hour," she said. "Just ten minutes to choose some paint for the house."

Slowly, Eve's guilt began to settle.

Inside, she felt as if the smallest jolt might shatter her completely. On a warm summer's end night, the boys played chase, happier than ever, while Jean and Eve sat watching them quietly.

"This land," Jean spoke. "It's all wrong. It's cursed somehow. It gets its hooks in and that's it. Something else lives here. This is its home, and it tricked you. Or at least, didn't tell you the full truth."

They did, I misunderstood. Or did I?

"Celeste told me they would take her. She said that, and I still did it. I thought she meant to take her to their world, I think. The Fae world. I led my mum to them," Eve answered.

I led her to be slaughtered.

"Maybe so, but I've been thinking. You led her there to save yourself and your brothers. You did to her what she did to your father."

"So, I deserve it happening to me, too? Maybe I did know, deep inside. Maybe I did know what they were going to do to her."

"No, Eve. You did it to save, she did it for spite and, I think, for money. She was rotten, rotten to the core and whatever lives out there knew it."

I did it because I wanted a life for myself. A happy life. I did it because I believed them. I believed Celeste, or whatever they are. Didn't I? Celeste loved me. I felt it.

"Where do you think she went after she… died?" Eve ventured.

"Wherever she deserved to be."

Eve didn't answer, couldn't. What could she say?

Instead, she watched her brothers play. With full stomachs and proper food, they had even more energy to burn.

Celeste, I miss her. I feel as if she's still here. We're linked together. I dream of her.

"Eve, help me decorate this place. Fix it up. It's been vile here for too long. Full of hate. Let's change that together. Let's make this cursed land good again."

Tears fell down her face, but still, Eve nodded.

"Aunt Jean, I feel as if I don't belong here. I never have. I feel like I belong with them. I just know it somehow."

"Nonsense child. Let's make it nice here, so you feel better."

That's not the answer, that's never going to be the answer.

The next two weeks brought more sunshine and heat. Eve played in the garden with her siblings. The house began to look cared for; the boys thrived.

The hollow feeling inside her did not fade. A piece of her was lost. She craved Celeste deeply. Missed the special bond that formed so quickly. She still felt like a stranger in her own body, in her own world.

The only thing that had ever felt right for her was being in the presence of Celeste.

On occasion, from the garden, she stopped to glance at the treeline. Towards the woods, the world she no longer dared to wander. Still, she felt the pull, the urge to venture back.

"Supper!" Jean called from the house. The boys raced in.

Eve lingered; a figure hidden within the trees caught her eye.

She saw a flash of blonde hair, the fabric of a deep red-colored dress.

Celeste, that's Celeste!

Slowly, she took a few steps forward, instantly pulled towards the girl.

NO! Don't! What if they kill me too?

She watched as the girl beckoned, called to her. She took another step forward, hypnotized, mesmerized, pulled, and lured.

I could just talk to her. That couldn't hurt. I need to see her so much.

Eve glanced back at the house. No one was watching. She darted quickly towards the trees and in.

"Celeste," she called.

The woodland appeared empty. Cautiously, she stepped in further.

"I know you're here," Eve whispered. "I can feel you."

Celeste giggled and appeared. She spun in a wild circle, her long red gown spread out around her. She stopped and smiled.

"Eight stones now. That means you have one more path. Care to peek without eyes?"

Another path!

"What are you?" Eve breathed.

"That depends on who it is that's doing the looking. It depends on what's inside them. Path eight, Eve. Look."

With quick light steps, she jumped forward and laid her delicate hands on Eve.

She closed her eyes. This time, she knew what to expect.

She saw herself in a new world, one of clear blue skies and ancient lush land. Her world but not; another layer, another hidden slice of existence.

Happy colorfully dressed people played wonderful soft-sounding music and ate fresh fruit under a perfectly pink sun. The emotions of love and bliss washed over her. It was a place like she imagined heaven might be. No war, no cruelty, no unhappiness, no hunger, no ruination, no pollution. Only love and friendship. Freedom and happiness. A different realm where each person was free to be themselves without judgment.

She saw herself laughing with Celeste, holding each other. The two of them, embracing, content together.

"Is this real? Or a trick?" Eve cried.

"No trick, a new path. You're a beacon. You can shine now. Come with me," Celeste smiled. "This is the way you see us; this is what you believe. This is what we are for you."

The woodland began to shimmer. A blur formed, warped like a circus mirror. A tone sounded. A single deep complex sound.

Celeste half stepped through the shimmer, into her world.

"Come," she said. "Please."

What should I do? I want to go.

Eve thought of her brothers, thought of her Aunt Jean.

It's not fair to hurt them, losing mum and then me? But... Celeste. I want to be with her. In her world, not this one.

"You are the Good folk," Eve whispered. "You are."

"Only for the beacons. Now please, the door is closing. Path eight Eve."

Celeste beckoned her, her small delicate hand opened for her.

I want this more than anything, should I? Can I?

"But my family!"

"We can erase. No one will remember you. You swapped, you paid. Quick, decide. Tick-tock."

Eve knew what and who she wanted in one moment of perfect singularity. No, she would not stay in a world that hurt her. She would not live an existence afraid to be who she was. She would not survive unwelcome. She knew her futures. Sorrow would kill her while happiness waited.

"Forgive me," Eve whispered.

She gripped the girl's hand and felt no shred of regret.

She laughed, an unfamiliar sound. A bubble of sheer joy rose up in her chest. Yes, she would be happy. She would be with Celeste. She had an opportunity, and she'd paid dearly for it. Perhaps her whole life had been payment. She stepped forward and vanished.

The girl that did not belong in the world she was born into was gone.

Two Hours Later

Jean walked through the woods. Occasionally, she stopped to shout for her niece. She called her name so many times her throat grew sore and scratched.

A deep feeling of dread sat in the bottom of her stomach. Silently, tears fell down her face.

I know it, I can feel it. She's gone.

As she came towards the stones, her growing suspicions turned to knowledge. She counted quickly, then twice more, slowly. She knew, without a doubt.

Nine stones. Nine stones now stood. No Eve, gone.

Jean sank to the ground, heart aching and hurt.

"Why Eve?" She shouted. "Why?"

She hardly needed to ask. She knew exactly why. Eve had tried hard to tell her, and she hadn't understood, she hadn't realized.

She sat and sobbed until her chest hurt and her eyes stung.

It was only minutes later when Jean began to wonder what on earth she was doing kneeling down in the woods.

She wondered if she'd been looking for something, if she had, she'd completely forgotten what it was.

"Silly old woman," she mumbled to herself.

Berries, it must have been berries she was searching for, after all, she promised she'd make a fresh pie with cream.

She wiped her stinging eyes. It must be hay fever again. Every summer was the same. She would go home and take her allergy medicine. Besides, she wanted to relax and make more plans to decorate the house. Maybe she would even bake cookies for the boys. They always loved sweet treats.

She hummed a lullaby as she walked back to the house that was now her home.

Story Notes

There is a beautiful stone circle in Derbyshire called The Nine Ladies standing stones. It is a wonderful place.

The idea for this story came from visiting those stones. I saw a lone girl wandering one day; she looked at home somehow, lost in her own world in the way only daydreamers can do. In my mind, I imagined she might be a magical being who chose to pop into our dimension for a peek. As it happens, she was as ordinary as me and parked next to my own car.

The swapping lady, the wild woman and the swapping concept, first appeared in Autumn of '79, in my short story collection, Paint it Black, where she met a group of children eager for a swap of their own.

Swaps and trades with a seemingly magical being from another realm.

Would you? Could you?

CAT MEAT WOMAN

1888 London

Ethel Taylor was better known around the streets of East End London as a cat meat man. Not a cat meat woman, for no one ever saw her as female or feminine in any way. She did not sell the meat of cats to unwary patrons eager for a meal, no; she sold cow, pig, and horse meat to the owners of cats, *for* cats.

Dregs and unwanted bits; she collected and brought, fresh from the many slaughterhouses that littered the areas, docks included.

Early every morning, she would leave her tiny room in her crumbling, damp boarding house, dressed in her tired old rag clothing and bloodied apron. She would arrive with her few precious shillings and pay to fill her rickety wooden cart with bloodied meat and still warm organs. Sometimes, the slaughtermen let her take a little marrow of the bone or a chewy piece of gristle for free, all the nasty bits the butchers would never be able to sell without a con.

No one ever paid her much mind. She was old and crooked, tired and silent.

Ethel hardly spoke. She saved her voice for very special occasions, which, for her, never seemed to occur.

She had been cursed with unfortunate facial features too, a very large and misshapen forehead and nose. Eyes that were not at all symmetrically placed and her teeth had long since crumbled away and fallen out. When she tried to smile, she sneered instead, and so she quit smiling altogether.

Ethel was viewed as nothing more than a rather harmless and tired old cat meat man, albeit a woman.

169

Yet she had old and dusty secrets. She was lonely, and bitterly so. She craved the company of a human being with fierce desperation. Yes, she enjoyed the friendship of the many cats who followed her all day long, after second and third helpings of meat, no doubt. And yes, she was fond of the stray dogs she often stopped to pat and feed with the special gristle or marrow bone.

But none gave her the love she needed, the attention or companionship she yearned for. Even the birds she fed on occasion only wanted her for her precious scraps of bread. As soon as her bread was gone, they too left her.

Sometimes she would sit in the big green park, eager to be around other people, until the Bobbies came, Peel's boys, the wretched police, and moved her away.

"You're ugly, you're unsightly," they'd jeer at her. "This park is for ladies and gentlemen, not a cat meat man. Go on, scram. You stink."

And off she'd go. Shuffling away, shame filling her face and with a trail of cats walking behind her.

It was a shame. She liked to stare at couples walking arm in arm while she wondered why she couldn't be one of them. Life, by all accounts, hadn't been fair to her by giving her no one to share her worries or woes with.

She took to sitting in the local cemetery whenever her old knees felt as if they might buckle and give up, which was often. Where else could she go when no one wanted her, except to the quiet dead.

The cats, those clever and crafty felines, took to waiting patiently for her. A whole clowder of them sat on fancy headstones and watched out for her. She tried to give them names but forgot who was who. Besides, they already had titles and owners, pretty collars too. They had more love in their furry lives than she did.

Ethel also had in her possession two old coins of God only knew from where. Her own mother had pressed those coins into her small hands years before as she was dying of consumption.

"Wish coins, these are," she'd said in her gravelly death rattle. "Last chance wishes."

Ethel had no real idea what it all meant, or why her mother hadn't used the wishes for herself. It seemed a logical conclusion, but then her mother hadn't been the brightest of folks. She kept her coins for a special day when she felt she might have no real options left but to make a wish.

One afternoon, as she sat resting in the cemetery and shooing the greedy cats away, a funeral occurred. She was in a posh area, a place she really had no business being in. Yet she was tucked out of sight, only the corner of her cart was in view, and no one paid much attention.

The cat meat woman hit upon an idea as the sleek box was lowered into the ground.

A body.

It was going to get bitterly cold soon and her joints suffered terribly in winter. She barely made enough money to keep paying for her lodgings, and certainly not enough for a fourth or fifth-hand wool coat to keep her warm.

All of the clothes she was wearing were stolen straight from piles of rubbish, thrown out by wealthy people with more money than sense. Even her boots were odd and mismatched, but no one noticed. No one ever did. Besides, was it stealing when the person didn't want the belongings anymore? No, she thought not.

But a body; could she do it?

She was strong. There was no doubt about that. Years of pushing a bloody cart filled with fresh hearts and livers saw to giving her muscle. She could be quick and stealthy, too. The streets of London were a dangerous place, after all, and she knew how to keep her wits about her.

But where would she keep a corpse? Her boarding house was revolting. Covered in filth and with a nosey woman running the whole place. No, there were some rotten types that would likely spoil things for her and pry into her business.

What about that old wooden shed no one used?

She knew it well; she lived in the shed the summer before. It sat on a patch of wasteland and got the same amount of attention she did, which was none.

Cat meat woman smiled. Perhaps she wouldn't need to be so lonely soon.

A line of cats followed her to the shed the very next day. She'd finished her round and sold everything she'd got from the slaughterhouse. She'd saved a bone all for herself, so she could suck the marrow straight out. She swore such a thing could ward off illnesses, but did anyone listen? No. They never did.

The shed was in a worse state than it was the year before. It was barely standing, and it would be hard work to put it right. It would take money she didn't have. Salvaged wood and nails, that's really all it needed. Just a little something to keep the cold air out.

It took weeks to find everything she needed, and even then she had to stuff old rags into gaps and cracks in the shoddy walls. It was a hovel, but a private one.

She had nothing to pack at the boarding house, no belongings of her own, and so she simply failed to return. No doubt her room was filled by the end of the night or the next one.

Two nights she spent inside the shed, shivering. She was waiting on a full moon before she set off to commit her vile act. There were rules to those wishes, she remembered. She was no fool and besides; she had great plans.

Darkness was her cover, her thing to hide behind. Out of her shed, she came creeping. Just like all the other nasty slithering things at night.

"Meow."

She tutted. Of course, cats. They had comfortable homes with warm fireplaces, yet they expected her to have meat at the ready and so she had become their parent somehow. A sliver of heart or kidney was preferable to warmth for them. Well, no matter. They were free creatures in a sense, they could do what they wanted, just like her.

The cemetery was her aim, her singular purpose. She pushed her empty cat meat cart along with her, the wheel squeaking as she went, coughing into the thick smog.

The streets were almost dead, a few homeless opened an eye as she passed by.

They only saw a poor and crooked cat meat man, nothing important.

A few drunkards caught sight of her. But no, only a cat meat man, no one they could bother for fun or rob for a decent sum.

Creak, creak, creak. She walked along largely unseen, shielded by night.

A large man stood alone in the cemetery, no light around him. But she saw him clearly enough. The moon helped her see the important things.

She coughed to clear her dry throat; it was vital she found her voice. Arranging such a meeting hadn't been easy.

"Ain't no Bobbies 'round is there? No filth?" The gruff voice spoke as soon as she got close.

She shook her head.

"Whaddaya' want with this anyhow? Gonna sell it?"

At the man's feet lay a fresh, sheet wrapped body. She had no choice but to arrange for such a thing. Strength was one thing, but digging six feet down required more muscle than she possessed, and also a spade.

Ethel did not answer the man. The man she first found selling stolen items down a back alley.

Instead, she reached into her pocket and removed a gold-colored coin. One of the two she possessed.

The man snatched the coin greedily and held it up to the moonlight. He grunted and bit down sharply on the object.

"Got any more, 'ave ya'?" He asked.

She shook her head in reply.

"Ya' ain't lyin' is ya'?"

Again, a head shake.

"Better be real or I'll come for ya'. Get it? An' you'll be cat meat, I'll see to it."

Ethel nodded to show she understood. She lowered her head briefly and when she raised it again, the man was gone. Off to hide in shadows and commit wild sins, no doubt.

It hadn't been as hard as she expected, finding someone to dig up a corpse. Men did it all the time, to sell cadavers to infirmaries and whatnot.

Shame about the coin, though. Still, there was one left, and that was what mattered. One was all she needed.

The journey home, back to the shed, was treacherous. Her cart wobbled badly with such a bulky item wedged inside. The shape looked too much like a dead body and this worried her greatly.

A string of cats followed her and only paused to hiss and wag their tails when a lone Bobby blew his whistle and came barrelling towards her.

"What's that ya' got?" He yelled.

"Cat meat."

"You a cat meat man?"

"Yes."

"That don't look like no cat meat."

Ethel took a deep breath. It wasn't possible that she could run. Even if she dropped the cart, she'd never make it far. She would be hanged and then what? She'd die as she lived, all alone but with a rope around her neck for company and a jeering crowd watching her demise.

"Meow. Meow. Meow."

A chorus of cats erupted. Several began to circle her in solidarity.

"See. Cat meat," she repeated.

"Get outta here," the officer growled. He appeared not to be fond of cats and that made Ethel hate him even more. "Take those fuckin' pests with ya'. Fuckin' vermin, the lot of ya'."

She pushed on with her cart and smiled. She would reward the cats with extra kidney chunks as a special treat for saving her literal neck.

The day passed quickly; she did her rounds and fed her animal friends well. She collected her few shillings and saved them for the next day. No one paid her any attention. She was, after all, a harmless cat meat man dressed in a bloody apron.

As soon as she arrived back at her shed, she got to work.

The body was not as fresh as she wanted, but it would have to do. The skin was mottled, and the smell of the corpse was worse than the slaughterhouse she frequented. Still, the body of the man was in good shape, no missing limbs or pieces. She guessed he must have been loved by someone, and he looked handsome too. His headstone claimed he was a surgeon of some kind. She couldn't read all the words properly. She had no education, so she couldn't be sure.

His hands were strong and clever, that much she knew.

She washed him in slimy water, taken from a nearby pond, and sang an old folk song to him.

If everything worked as it should, and there was no reason it shouldn't, then she would soon have fine company. Perhaps his memories, or some of them, might even be intact?

Time to concentrate. She pricked her finger until a tide of blood popped up. She carefully wrote strange picture symbols, drawn from old memory, along with her wish, onto an old piece of newspaper. She forced the mouth of the corpse open and jammed the paper inside. Next, she placed her last gold coin alongside it and held the jaw shut.

A second prick to another finger and soon the body had strange shapes and symbols scrawled all over it.

She covered the corpse with rags and waited. That was all she could do. Wait for the magic to take effect. Wait for the unique wish coin and special symbols to revive him.

Cat meat woman lay down next to him and felt nothing but cold from his body.

She shivered deeply.

"Please work," she said aloud. "I do wish it."

Her voice hurt from being used so much in such little time, but she hoped it would all be worth it.

She was lonely. So very lonely. She only wanted a friend.

Yet no life coursed through the body, no surge of magical power. The corpse remained still and utterly dead.

Dawn arrived and brought with it a fierce chill in the air.

Ethel felt frozen and defeated. Her limbs and joints hurt from lack of warmth or a bed of any kind.

She had to get up; she had to earn enough to keep herself fed and feed the cats.

What use was saving a coin her own mother had promised her was magical? What a fool she was to believe such nonsense. Perhaps she should have sold it. Wishes were lies.

She turned behind her. The man was still lifeless. Yes, it was all for nothing.

Later, when she was back, she told herself she would take the coin out of the corpse and pawn it. It might make her enough to find a bed in a better boarding house, if only for a week.

Up she got, walking the streets of London with her cart full of fresh cat meat.

She stopped briefly to feed a few stray dogs and scratch one good boy behind the ears.

She saw the look in his eyes and understood completely. She gave him the special marrow bone she was saving for herself.

Perhaps she could keep the dog? Perhaps he could be her company? Yet he was part of a pack of strays, and they all looked out for each other. Was she part of a pack or a clowder of cats? A murder of crows? No. Not even part of a pair, and it just wasn't right.

Was it her fate to be so alone and spend her short remaining years delivering bloody meat all by herself? Until she died from the cold that was coming? Perhaps the cats would eat her, and she would truly become a cat meat woman, with her own meat for their food.

She thought hard as she shuffled back to her shed. And what about the body? What would she do with it? Maggots and flies would come and find him. They always had a skill for finding the best meat for miles, and he would smell much worse very soon.

She would have to slide him into the pond and never fetch water from there again, lest it be cursed.

When she got back to her small shed, her hovel. The body was gone.

At first, the cat meat woman panicked.

Now she would be for it. Before she knew what was happening, she would be hanging from those terrible gallows or losing her head.

It occurred to her that the shady character she found down the back alley, the man who dug up the body for a gold coin, must have followed her that first night and snatched him clean away, likely to sell to a hospital, cadaver trade. Which meant he had both of her special wish coins, too.

She sat on the floor and cried, more alone than ever. Her temporary friends, the cats, circled her, drawn by her scent of rotten meat, and seeking to offer comfort in the only way they knew how.

"All for nowt'," she whispered. "It was all for nowt."

Her sorrow became too much to bear. She could die right now, and no one would miss her. The cats might, but a new cat meat man would snatch her route and they would follow him instead like a pied piper led by their full bellies.

Misery. It was all she'd ever known. London was a capital of all that was unjust and unfair. This, she knew. She fell asleep where she lay. Curled up and cold. Winter was on its way. Jack Frost himself was getting ready. She knew the bitter cold would kill her. She wondered if she even cared.

When she woke, she assumed she was still dreaming.

A body was pressed up against her back and she was warm. Toasty warm like never before. A heavy arm was slung around her waist. A human arm, with pretty clever hands.

"What!" She gasped. She rolled away and scraped her body across the hard floor.

It was him. The body was breathing. He was alive.

Sleeping, yes, but alive all the same.

She poked his arm. Warm. Soft. Vibrant.

Somehow, he'd even managed to find clothing. He wore a black outfit and a warm cape coat. He looked smart and handsome, even in his dreams. And he'd returned to her, wherever he'd been. He understood they were bound.

"Hello," she dared to say. No answer. Only a flicker of movement from underneath his eyelids.

It was a miracle. Intervention of the divine kind. A revival of life.

A spell and wish, but one of light and not darkness. The coin really was magical. It was the only answer.

Ethel placed her hand over her mouth in utter shock and laughed. The sensation felt brand new to her. So much so that it hurt her face to smile with unused muscles.

Finally, she had someone. A man to share her life with. A companion who would talk to her and tell her things. Perhaps he could even tell her about the world and every wonderful thing it was said to contain.

A pile of coins sat near the door, a big pile. Big enough that she didn't have to sell cat meat that day.

Ethel was very happy indeed. She curled up next to him, safe and warm. Almost purring like the cats she fed.

***

He would only wake at night and even then, he insisted on leaving, although he always returned. Like her, he chose not to speak. He communicated with his eyes, although little more than cloudy dead orbs. He would nod or shake his head. Yes or no.

She knew not his name nor why his longing to leave every night was so fierce. She was grateful at least that together; they had found proper lodgings. She had a roof without holes over her head and walls around her. Safety and warmth, every day. They even had a fireplace, a luxury in the hovels of Whitehall. Old Jack Frost could touch neither of them.

When word of the killings began to spread, close to where the two lived, she remained silent.

Women of the night were being slaughtered, a ripper was on the loose, a brutal slicer of flesh and body. Still, she remained tight-lipped.

When he returned home dressed in bloody clothing, she helped bathe him and wash the stains from his outfit. When Bobbies searched for a man matching his description, she shook her head. She knew nothing; she was only a cat meat woman. What did she know?

No one paid any attention to her, anyway. No one ever did.

She discovered he had hidden body parts under the floorboards, wrapped in old cloth. She tutted, yes, but added the curious parts to her cat meat cart to be rid of such things.

She decided they would save up and move away. He always brought home plenty of coins. Sharp knives too. Ones she had to be very careful to clean. Perhaps they could board a great ship and sail to the new world. She always wanted to see such a place and once there, they could be anyone.

She guessed the man, Jack, for she named him after the papers christened him, had not returned as complete or as the man he once was in life, or perhaps something else returned in his place to animate his body.

But what did it matter? No one had ever cared for her. Why should she care for them?

What was important was that she wasn't alone. That's what truly mattered. No, she would never be alone again. She had a friend, and she was good at keeping secrets.

Finally, the cat meat woman knew happiness.

Story Notes

I adore documentaries, or brain food as I call them. One documentary about life in Victorian Britain caught my attention solely for mentioning cat meat men. I found the concept fascinating, that there had truly been such a profession. It sounded funny and charming to me in a way. Although, of course, very difficult and gore-filled.

Still, if I ever happen to give up my work in healthcare, I will no doubt be found pushing a wooden cart around, piled high with meat and feeding all the neighborhood cats.

TWILIGHT

Eighty-two-year-old Ken Reynolds almost falls asleep in his special armchair, the fancy leather one that has a special button to help him stand.

He hasn't been up and out of bed for long. It's the painkillers that cause his drowsiness. Yes, they work a little and help ease the vivid brutality inside him, but they make him tired too. He likes sleeping a great deal. He'll admit that to anyone, yet he is a man living on borrowed time. He needs all the hours awake he can get.

There is still a lot to do.

Cancer. It's ravaging his body. Eating him away and he feels certain he can feel every single bite the wicked disease takes of him.

He promises himself he will have five more minutes of thinking time before he gets started. Today is an important day. It could well be *the* day.

He still needs two more new tires, but thanks to his grandson, David, they should be arriving very soon. At least, he thinks so. David always told him he could track anything down on that fancy interweb thingy and he was right.

As soon as those two new tires are on. Ken plans to take a drive. Just one last drive before he dies. Down the long road, close to his driveway, and back again.

It's his last wish. He's spent nearly his whole life with that car, and she has a mind of her own. He could swear to it. Not cells and neurons, no, but moving parts and living energy.

He leans back in his chair and thinks about the day he first saw her. It is one of his most favorite memories to retrieve from his own mind's database.

Gosh, she was a beauty. Nearly as stunning as Bella, the woman he fell in love with and proudly married.

He loves the car almost as much as he loved his precious wife.

Poppy, that's what he named her. On account of her being a Ford Popular and the car really is a she, he was able to sense such a thing from the very beginning.

***

He was working as a milkman when Poppy first caught his eye, back in sixty-three when he was just twenty. He had no great aspirations in life, no real ambition. He was content as he was earning the amount he did.

His delivery route took him past a big car showroom twice a day. There she sat, all shiny and blue and with a sticker stuck to her windshield that was astronomically far out of his price range. The first time he laid his eyes on her, he almost crashed. In fact, four milk bottles smashed that day and fresh milk spilled all over. Boy, did he get into trouble for that, yet he wasn't upset.

No, he was captivated. Completely enthralled.

Twice a day he would drive past to wave at her.

Sometimes, he even parked up in his milk float so he could sit and stare at her. In his mind, he would imagine all the adventures they would have if he ever owned her. He would drive around proudly and take the very best care on the roads. He would wash her twice a day if she needed it and change her oil and water whenever she grew short.

The milk round didn't bring in enough money to buy such a beauty. He took a job cleaning a school in the evenings and took on as much overtime as he could manage.

Still, not enough money. Not even close.

Then one day, she was gone. Vanished from the spot that seemed to be her own.

Ken pulled his float over and panicked. Had someone with more money than him come along and purchased her? The feeling inside him was brutal. The cold and bitter knowledge that he would never get to own her or drive her hit him in painful waves. He had lost something that was never his.

No one else would take care of her the way he would. He knew it.

Yes, he might be able to afford a brand-new Ford someday, but it had to be her. She was meant to be his, and he felt it with every core of his being.

His feet moved before he became aware of what was happening. Into the showroom, he walked.

"The blue Ford Popular," he said. "Is it sold?"

"No," said the smart young salesman with the posh accent. "Something's wrong with the vacuum wipers. It's got to go back."

It! It's got to go back? He thought. How dare he refer to her as an it. And if she went away, how would he ever find her again?

No, it just wouldn't do.

"I'll buy her. It, I mean, I'll buy it."

"Sir, the vacuum wipers are broken. Other parts are faulty too."

"Then I'll replace them myself."

And why not? He liked tinkering with engines and greasy oil never bothered him. Besides, they were bound to be only small faults.

"Well, if you're sure," the salesman grinned, clearly eager for a sale. "I can't give you a discount."

"Oh, I'm sure," Ken said.

Now, he only needed the money. He called his parents and pleaded. The answer was a firm no. He had only one option left.

A bank loan.

Destiny arranged for the loan officer to be in the greatest mood of his life that same day. The stars lined up and collided, just for Ken.

The funds were soon in his account; the money was soon in the hands of the happy salesman; and Poppy, she was finally his.

The moment he drove away, the very moment he put his key in the ignition, he sensed a bond connecting him to the car. A tie to bind him firmly, a solid link. One that would grow and never fray or snap.

He was hers and she was his and Ken had never felt such happiness in his entire life. He drove every place he could think of. He purchased a map, and on his days, off, he proudly drove to rural places.

He never liked to park and leave his Poppy. He sat in his vinyl seat and ate a packed lunch instead.

The happy couple existed in harmony and the vacuum wipers didn't fail him once, and nor did any other parts.

A year to the day later, on a rainy afternoon, he splashed a lone woman, quite by accident, as she walked down a street. In fact, he was almost certain the car decided to swerve and hit the puddle on purpose.

He wound down his window and apologized.

"I'm sorry," he said.

"I should think you are!" The young woman smiled. "Oh! I like your car."

That was the moment he met Bella. His beautiful wife, the woman who came to love his car as much as he.

The trio enjoyed many drives and adventures together. Many repairs and replacement parts, many nights parked up, enjoying the view of the stars overhead.

On occasion, Poppy would refuse to start, especially on cold days. He would talk to her kindly and ask nicely. Without fail, she would start when she was good and ready.

Two days after Ken paid off his bank loan, he won a large amount of money. A perfect surprise. Priorities came first, a garage for his Poppy and a new ring for his Bella.

***

Ken sits in his comfy chair and daydreams. He half wishes he could have his time all over again. The one thing in his life that has been the ultimate pleasure, and just for him, was that car.

Yes, life has been good. He has been lucky, and he knows it.

He has two sons and one of his sons gifted him with a grandson he adores. As luck, or maybe fate, would have it, that grandson became an excellent mechanic.

He's been kind, always. He's been a good father and a good husband. He prides himself on such things.

Bella is gone. Her final days were spent inside the walls of a hospice. Stolen from him by the same illness that ravages his own body now.

He misses her with every breath, every second of life.

And all that money. He was smart. He invested the majority of it, and it grew. Within the last couple of years, it's been used, every single penny.

He divided up the sum for several charities and insisted upon secret donations to local families he knew were struggling. He put aside money for his own family, too. The last of it, a small amount, had been spent on his personal project.

The restoration of Poppy.

Long before Bella died, the car had been sitting inside his garage, tired out and done for. His son told him repeatedly that she was only good for scrap metal and salvaged parts. He refused to accept such cold words and refused to abandon her. And so, his grandson and he attempted to restore her.

Attempted being the word needed.

She was rustier than an old tin can left out in years of rain. The blue paintwork was all but destroyed and she hadn't been able to start for years. The windshield was cracked and there was a vicious dent in her bonnet.

A new engine was essential. A new heart. A transplant, or she wouldn't have a chance of starting up.

David and a few of his friends managed to install such a thing while Ken sat in the corner and happily watched his old girl become temporarily revived.

"One drive, Grandad, and she'll fall apart. The bodywork is…"

Yes, he knew. She was as infected with rot as he.

"That's fine, one drive is all I want, Lad. Just one."

"We'll need new brakes and tires."

"Shoes, and yes, do it. Do anything."

Tires for Poppy were always called new shoes. But even if the car was at its very basic core and likely dangerous to drive too, he still yearned to recall the blissful feeling of freedom she gave, that wonderful joy. He knew the link still existed between them; he could feel it just as powerful as ever.

One drive. Just one drive and he'd be happy.

The doorbell rings.

Ken usually hears the delivery men coming up his long and spiraling driveway and crunching all the gravel, but he heard no one. He must have fallen asleep after all, lost inside his carefully stored memories and daydreams. Sometimes, he forgets he is an old, poorly and exhausted man. Who was supposed to be bringing the vital tires? David or a delivery person?

"Hello?" he yells.

He can't miss a tire delivery. He just can't. It's far too important.

He inches forward in his seat and holds on tightly to his recliner button. He can't stand unaided; he needs the essential chair to help lift him.

"Leave them outside!" He tries to shout, but his voice is frail.

The doorbell rings again, and he feels a jolt of panic. He won't make it, he won't.

Finally, he is vertical, almost. He grabs his walking frame and begins his crucial steps.

Please wait, he thinks. *Please.*

Delivery drivers are always in a rush.

If those tires go back to the depot, he'll never track them down, and ringing up is no use. It's always a machine on the other end nowadays, a robot voice that sends his mind in a tangle.

I'm not going to make it in time.

Pain burst out inside him. He can feel the tumor spreading its tentacles of hate throughout his body. The agony makes him breathless and weaker than he already is.

An enemy inside.

He hears a key inside the lock of his front door.

"David?"

"Grandad, where are you? I've got the tires, well, the wheels. Sorry, no. Shoes!"

Ken sighs with relief and begins to laugh. Hope rises.

Today really is the day.

He feels both excited and anxious.

He wishes he could jump up and down, but he understands that trying such a thing will likely result in two broken hips or worse.

"How long now?" He asks his grandson. He has asked the same question ten times or more.

"About five minutes."

How can he wait five more minutes! His stomach is flipping all of its own accord and his legs are shaking. He pats the boot of his precious Poppy.

"Not long now," he whispers.

A ripple of pain erupts inside him. He gasps with shock and tries hard to ignore it. He doesn't want a painkiller to dull his feelings. He's waited years for this moment.

He can hear David turning a ratchet around and around. Bolts and screws litter the garage floor. Ken hopes the car won't collapse and fall apart the moment the jack is released.

"That's the wheels on as tight as I can get them."

"Now look, Poppy," Ken whispers. "You've got a fancy pair of new shoes."

A cold thought numbs him.

"Have we got petrol?" He asks.

"Course we have," David chuckles. "I got some from the garage on the way over."

"Good lad, you've been good to me."

"You're my grandad," David says. As if no further explanation is needed and perhaps one isn't.

"Are you sure you can do this?" He adds. "You look a bit…"

"I'm sure."

"We're not telling my dad about this, are we?"

"No, Lad. We're not," Ken laughs.

"Good. Right, underneath is really rotten. It's best to get going, and come to a natural stop before you get to the slope."

Ken feels grateful he has the longest driveway around. Bella always loved her privacy. He has her to thank for such a blessing. He can't drive on a road, not only will his Poppy not make it, but his eyesight won't, and his license is long since expired.

David speaks the magic words he has been waiting for.

"Right, Grandad. All done."

The garage door is open. The wheels are fitted, and the sun is shining brightly. Ken takes a deep breath to hold the agony inside as David helps him sit down comfortably. The driver's seat is still the original and although ripped and torn, it fits him like an old and comfortable glove.

He lifts his legs inside and grimaces at the effort.

"Are you okay?"

Ken is more than okay. He is where he always belonged.

Once, Poppy broke down near a picturesque reservoir. Her insides were always simple to fix, but Ken could see nothing wrong.

They were delayed by ten minutes or so. When she finally started, he saw a lorry had turned over miles down the road home.

Ken believes the car knew something of the danger ahead and had worked hard to prevent them from moving and becoming caught up in the wreck.

Of course, he told no one of his wild ideas. The secret stayed between the car and owner.

Even years later in both of their lives, in thick winter, he would think of her alone in the garage, cover her in a blanket and make sure she was still snug and safe on a daily basis.

Bella never minded. She would smile and roll her pretty blue eyes. They would joke and say the car was their very first child.

One year, she even knitted the car a blanket of red and white…

"Grandad?"

"Oh, yes. Sorry Lad, I'm fine. Good to go."

How easy it is to become lost in old, dusty thoughts.

"Shall I push you?"

"No, let's see if she starts."

David closes the car door with a gentle shove. There is no seat belt to fasten. When Poppy was made in sixty-two, there was no seatbelt law.

He holds the key in his shaking hand and pushes it into the ignition.

"Come on girl," he says. "One last adventure, just me and you."

He turns the key.

The engine sputters and dies.

"Come on, come on."

Images flood his mind, of all the times he pleaded and begged her to start. Cold mornings, damp mornings. He and Bella would always joke that Poppy needed a lie in.

"Come on Poppy, my old girl."

Please, please, please. One last drive.

He tries again and the engine fires.

"Woah!" David yells in triumph. A boom erupts from the exhaust pipe, but Ken is laughing far too hard to hear it.

He jerks forward and presses down on the accelerator, praying his foot doesn't go through the entire floor.

He is moving. Poppy is moving and quite suddenly he is the happiest man who ever lived.

He steers a little, his muscle memory flooding back.

"Remember when we drove to Scotland on a whim!" He chuckles. "And back again! And that time I reversed into a tree, and you were unhappy with me and wouldn't start!"

His eyesight is not perfect, in fact, it is quite terrible. All he can see is the cracks in the windshield and the glare of the hot sun and yet he feels confident, he feels wild. Pure and more real than he has for years.

He is no longer an old and frail man; he feels young once more.

"Oh Poppy," he says. He grips the steering wheel tightly, wishing he could drive for hours or days.

The radio clicks on of its own accord, an upgrade he made years before, compelled by the desire to give his car a voice.

The song *Twilight Time* begins to play.

Ken feels a shiver. This was his wedding song, the first song he ever truly loved.

A tear runs down his face. His vision blurs further. He blinks rapidly to clear his sight.

"I'm a silly old fool," he says.

The car stops and grinds to a halt.

"No! Not yet, please. Come on, girl. A bit further."

Wait! What is that sound?

What did I do?

Creaking and grinding metal. Is she falling apart? The noise becomes so loud, so quickly that he cringes. The cracking of glass follows. He braces for impact, except nothing happens. No glass explodes onto his lap. Only silence follows.

He dares to open one eye; suddenly sure his precious car and best friend is about to burst into wild flames.

He watches in amazement as the windscreen straightens. All the cracks vanish as if rubbed out by an unseen eraser.

The dent in the bonnet, gone.

The steering wheel he holds feels brand new. His seat buckles, rips heal, stitching tightens until it feels as firm as it did years before. "What!"

The vibrant blue paint is back, all shiny and bright, along with the wonderful scent of a brand-new car.

The dashboard is gleaming, the mileage registers zero.

Ken feels his heart thud rapidly. This can't be happening. He must be in some kind of painkiller induced fantasy.

Poppy starts. The engine roars to life. She sounds just as she always did. Loud and powerful. She feels as new as when he drove her away from that showroom the very first day.

He feels the force, the curious energy she always had. She is back and no longer only fit for scrap. No longer an old girl.

The windscreen wipers tick back and forth. They are not needed, there is no rain, she is happy; it is her equivalent of a dog wagging its tail.

Ken can't contain himself. He sobs openly, tears pouring. He never believed in magic, and yet what else can this be? It's a miracle, that's what. If it's a hallucination, it is utterly wonderful.

He laughs, full of joy.

Poppy sets off at speed. He is delirious, the most wonderful feeling he ever felt in his life. Shooting stars and happiness are bursting from his heart.

A shape catches his eye and only now does he truly understand. Bella. She is by his side in the seat she loved, smiling.

"Bella," he gasps. She looks glorious. His voice cracks with deep emotion.

The pain and agony inside him ceases to exist. One look in his rear-view mirror tells him why.

His hair is no longer white, his deep wrinkles are gone.

His skin is smooth, and his hair is brown, his eyes are clear and focused. He is young once more.

Bella reaches for his hand. The three of them are back together, finally. They will have the very best of last drives.

***

David runs full speed down the driveway. He is at a loss. The car stopped. Has the engine failed? Or the brakes caught?

Black smoke was pouring out, yes, but still, the car should be running a little. It was a fourth or fifth hand engine, but it worked.

"Grandad?" He yells.

Did he press down on the accelerator too much, or destroy the clutch? The car was so knackered that the slightest touch could have damaged it.

"Grandad," he repeats as he gets close.

There is no answer. His grandfather is still. There is no movement.

David sees his body, he looks as if he fell asleep at the wheel, except he is smiling, and his face is wet with tears.

"No," he says. "No, no, please!"

He can't think of anything else to say. He pulls at the car door and opens it, his own eyes blurred with tears.

But what should he do? Pull his grandad out and try CPR or leave him alone?

He reaches for his phone; he needs to call his dad and an ambulance. His grandad's heart must have given out. He is, no, was, very, very sick and in pain.

"Grandad?" He sobs.

David decides to leave him alone, at peace. He has died naturally doing what he loves. It wouldn't be right to move him. It would be an act of cruelty.

He crouches down and retches. Sorrow and grief overwhelms him.

He can hear the strains of the song *Twilight Time* playing on the car radio. He knows the song, it's his Grandad's favorite.

David stops and shuffles backward, immediately spooked. A sudden realization makes him jolt.

His grandad always said the car has a life of its own. He can believe it now.

He has to.

After all, the radio isn't even connected…

Story Notes

For all the dark stories I tend to write, I also like simple little tales like this, however predictable.

The idea came as I was again, out walking my lovely dog.

I am very hard of hearing but I heard the sound of a large engine of some kind; it was so loud! Fearing I was about to be squished by a falling jet engine, I looked up.

Only my dog had enough common sense to look behind us.

A beautiful blue colored Ford Popular came up the country road, looking as vibrant as if it were brand new. Yet what really caught my attention was the elderly man in the passenger seat. The look of sheer and complete joy on his face made me smile so much it hurt my own face. He was half hanging out of the window like an excited dog on a car journey. There was a man who was recalling his own youth, his very own adventures, and what a wonderful sight it was. It made me happy all the way into my bones and sometimes we all need a little of that in our lives.

I hope you have enjoyed this collection. Any proceeds will go to charity as always. Much love and thank you.

Printed in Great Britain
by Amazon